ABOUT THE AUTHOR

James Warden was a teacher for forty years and retired in 2006. He now enjoys his retirement as much as he enjoyed his time in the education service and is catching up on those things which he left undone and ought to have done – in particular, his writing. He writes every morning between nine o'clock and noon, for thirty-six weeks of the year.

He is fortunate enough to be able to act in several Norwich theatres – the Maddermarket, the Sewell Barn and, with the Great Hall Players, at the Assembly House – and this experience informs his writing. His stage adaptation of Laurie Lee's *As I Walked Out One Midsummer Morning* was performed at the Sewell Barn Theatre in November 2009. His original play, *Letters from a Boy in the Trenches*, which was based on the letters of a WW1 soldier, was performed in Marchington, Staffordshire in 2015.

James is married – for the second time – and lives in Norfolk. He and his wife travel as much as possible. They have visited Italy (where they were married in 2002) several times, Canada, Bermuda, Egypt, India, the Czech Republic, New England, Poland, Slovenia, Antarctica, the Falkland Islands, Alaska, the Galapagos Islands, Australia and Switzerland. In 2018, they travelled across the USA on Route 66. They have also taken several holidays in various Mediterranean resorts – the basis for his first novel, *Three Women of a Certain Age*, which was published in July 2010.

During his years in education, he wrote about twenty play scripts for children. These included the one that formed the basis for his children's story, *The Great Gobbler and his Home Baking Factory at the North Pole*, which he wrote in 1982 and published in December 2010.

He has three sons by his first marriage, and they inspired three of his novels – *The Vampire's Homecoming,* published in 2011, *The One-eyed Dwarf,* published in 2012 and *The Haunting of Thornham Staithe,* published in 2022. With them and his first wife, he also travelled to the southern states of North America, France, Germany (West and East), Estonia and what was Czechoslovakia.

WRITING BY JAMES WARDEN

Stories of Our Time
Three Women of a Certain Age (2010)
The Age of Wisdom (2015))
Swinging in the Sixties (2016)

'Tales of Mystery and Imagination'
The Vampire's Homecoming (2011)
The First Rendlesham Incident (2017)
The Search for Edwin Drood (2020)
The Haunting of Thornham Staithe (2022)

Stories for Children
The Great Gobbler and his Home-Baking Factory
at the North Pole (2010)
The One-eyed Dwarf (2012)

Biography
The Boy in the Photograph: Bill Pieri's
autobiography (2014)
A Child of the Fifties: autobiography of my
childhood (2017)

Plays
As I Walked Out One Midsummer Morning
*(Adapted with the permission of Laurie Lee's estate
and performed at the Sewell Barn Theatre in
Norwich in November 2009.)*

Letters from a Boy in the Trenches
*(Adapted from the letters home of Sydney
Harrison and performed by the Marchington
Amateur Dramatic Society in November 2015.)*

The Bingham Detective Stories
Bingham's First Case (2018)
Bingham and the Runaway Wife (2019)
Bingham and the Odd Couple (2020)
Bingham and the Minister's Clerk (2021)
Bingham and the Traveller's Daughter (2022)
Bingham Along the Stuart Highway (2023)
Bingham Goes to Cannes (2024)
Bingham and the Lost Years
(To be published in 2025)
Bingham Crosses the Bar
(To be published in 2026)
Bingham's Dog Fight
(To be published in 2027)
Bingham's Cambridge Christmas
(To be published in 2028)
Bingham in Prison
(To be published in 2029)

BINGHAM GOES TO CANNES

BY

JAMES WARDEN

Grosvenor House
Publishing Limited

This book is published by
Grosvenor House Publishing Ltd
Link House
140 The Broadway, Tolworth, Surrey, KT6 7HT.
www.grosvenorhousepublishing.co.uk

This book is a work of fiction. Any resemblance to
people or events, past or present, is purely coincidental.

A CIP record for this book
is available from the British Library

ISBN 978-1-80381-859-7

Chapter One
THE CHILD

Had Lina not been contacted by an old flame and invited to the Cannes Film Festival, and had Bingham, unlike his wife, not been refused an accreditation badge, he would not have found himself sitting in the shaded, grassy patch outside the café watching the little boy.

*

Neither one of the Binghams had expected a holiday that year, let alone one paid for by Patrizio Lucatti, one-time director of operas and one-time lover of Lina; but once the invitation arrived, it seemed churlish to refuse the kindness that was assumed to have been intended. Bingham would have been quite happy for Lina to go alone, but she insisted that he go with her.

"Why?"

"You know why, and I'm saying no more."

"The invitation was addressed to you."

"It implied both of us."

"That's not how I read it. It's only you who'll have this badge you need to get into the film previews."

"We'll find you one when we get there."

The discussion could have continued far into the day but Bingham rather liked France and had never been to

Cannes – at least, not to stay; besides, he could see that his wife was more than a little agitated at the thought of being alone among the illuminati, and with an old admirer.

As a young woman, she showed promise as an opera singer and, following three years of study at the Royal Northern College of Music, won a scholarship in 1970 to study with Carla Moscardini in Rome. It was there she met Patrizio, also a student and destined to become a leading light in the Italian operatic world. With him and other students she toured Italy and performed in Lucca, Verona, Florence, Venice and Rome itself. Both she and Patrizio were especially fond of the works of Puccini and it was a film of the great composer's life on which Patrizio was an executive producer and consultant that brought him to Cannes in the May of 2018.

*

On that particular morning, the morning Bingham first cast eyes on the little boy, Lina and Patrizio left him in the Café Potiniere and sauntered off to their first film showing – not the Puccini film but one in which a friend of Patrizio's had been involved. During their conversation over 'colazione', as Patrizio insisted on calling breakfast, showing little respect Bingham thought for their host country, Lina's admirer held forth on a range of topics, all of which led back, by whatever route, to himself.

Satisfied that his wife was in for an interesting morning, Bingham sauntered out to admire the seafront and the boats, when the little boy caught his attention, both the boy and the old woman. She had dumped, rather than sat, herself on one of the seats in the shade and was gazing, a troubled look in her expression, at the child who was pushing forward an inertia driven car and then racing to stop it running into the grass.

Bingham had a natural liking for children, even those he'd been obliged to discipline when he was a teacher; he sometimes thought *especially* those he'd had to discipline. They were vulnerable; it was that simple. Even the so-called 'streetwise kids' were awash in an adult world, often at the mercy of people, including their parents, who had little regard for their needs; and this was how the old woman struck him. She seemed to be responsible for the child but was drifting off into a world of her own.

Staring at them, Bingham decided there was more than just plain negligence at work with the pair: they didn't look as though they belonged together.

He sat down, foregoing his walk to the seafront, and waited. Sooner or later, something must happen to cause one or the other to speak.

The boy could not have been more than four or five years old. He was an attractive lad with large, green eyes that seemed to stare and smile at the same time: a boy who looked out on the world with a mixture of wonder and bewilderment. His ginger hair was short, cut neatly to the shape of his head – a head, Bingham decided, that held the promise of intelligence: the dome was large and extended at the back. Only the mouth troubled Bingham, immediately: it was tight, drawn in on itself. The way it turned up at one corner might have indicated truculence, but Bingham detected nerves.

He looked at the eyes again as the boy glanced up. There was apprehension there; Bingham was sure of the fact.

The old woman didn't move, not so much as to glance at Bingham. She sat collapsed on the bench, her eyes fixed on the child and the ground somewhere between the patch of grass and the pavement that separated their place of seclusion under the lime trees from the little slip of road that led down to La Croisette, the famous boulevard that runs the whole length of Cannes, separating the houses, hotels and restaurants from the beach, and which extends around the bay to the east of the port.

If only the boy would run the little car against Bingham's shoes, it would give him an excuse to speak, an excuse that would seem natural and unforced, not one that might rouse suspicions in a protective grandmother. Was the old girl the boy's grandmother? Bingham questioned his initial assumption that the two seemed worlds apart. If she wasn't, then she must surely be someone his parents trusted – mustn't she?

"Bonjour. C'est une belle voiture, vous avez," said Bingham, suddenly; surprising himself by a decision to speak that had been more instinctive than intended.

The little boy looked up and it was clear he was making an effort to understand what Bingham had said.

"That's a fine car, you have."

The boy smiled.

"When I was a boy, I had a car like that. It would make a whirring sound just like yours. I would push it along the floor and my mummy would turn it round and let it come back."

Although clearly interested the boy made no attempt to speak but looked up at the old woman as though seeking permission.

"Bonjour, Madame. Il est beau garcon."

The old lady smiled back, a tired smile but one that showed pride in the compliment Bingham paid.

Should he ask or would the question cause offence? After all, it was none of his business whether she was his grandmother or not. Bingham continued his smile and waited. At least, his greeting gave him an excuse to look her over.

She must have been well into her fifties, possibly older, and was fat; not grossly overweight like American and English women of a similar type and disposition, but fat nevertheless, comfortably fat like the older women Bingham remembered from his childhood, when no one seemed overweight until they reached a certain age. She was well-dressed, if clumsily so. Her clothes must have cost a good deal and were cut to conceal her belly. They were worn with a carelessness that denied the diligence inherent in their purchase.

She seemed neither poor nor well-to-do. Looking her in the eyes, Bingham decided she seemed beyond caring about much at all. It was as though she was waiting for something to happen, something quite beyond her control. But she was waiting for it, nonetheless, and with anticipation, as though it would bring her relief. Relief from what: a situation that was, or had become, unbearable?

Somehow, these feelings were centred on or around the child; and they were feelings that would concern only a woman. Later, reflecting on his thoughts when he sat under the shade of the lime trees, shielded from the sounds of the boulevard by the oleander bushes, Bingham would realise how near he came to the truth so early on.

"C'est une belle journée. Après la pluie, nous pouvons nous réjouissons du soleil."

After the rain, the sun! Talking about the weather was so English wasn't it? Bingham laughed at himself, and the old woman's eyes returned a faded sparkle, but she said nothing. She said nothing, but she smiled – almost – and Bingham seized his opportunity.

"Do you have lots of toys?" he asked the boy, translating for the woman.

The child nodded and smiled – almost.

"When I was your age, my favourite was a red fire engine. It wouldn't move on its own like your car, but sometimes I ran it down a plank of wood my dad had in the garden."

Having passed this piece of information on to the woman, Bingham waited. The boy would react, wouldn't he? Curiosity should provoke him, shouldn't it?

"What was the plank for?"

"My daddy used to kneel on it when he did the garden."

The boy frowned.

"The fire engine was quite big and had a ladder I could make go up by turning a wheel."

"Did the firemen go up the ladder?"

"There were four firemen. One was the driver, one pulled out the hose and one climbed the ladder."

The boy frowned again, and Bingham wondered whether he would make the obvious query. He did.

"What did the other man do?"

"He turned on the water tap."

"Why did your daddy kneel on the plank?"

"Because it hurt his knees if he didn't."

The boy laughed. It was a joyous sound, one almost of relief.

"My name's George," said Bingham, and held his breath.

He translated rapidly, meeting the grandmother's eyes every time, holding them and smiling. He didn't translate his last comment but waited. He couldn't ask, but would the boy respond?

"I have two little boys of my own. Well, they are not little any longer. One is a doctor and the other is a chemist."

Still Bingham did not translate.

"What are their names?"

"Paul and Benjamin, but we call Benjamin, Ben, and my wife calls Paul, Paolo."

"That's a funny name."

"It's Italian for Paul."

The old woman shifted on the seat. Bingham looked at her.

"Nous parlons de mes enfants," he said, not wanting to give any further information.

"Is your wife Italian?"

The question surprised Bingham. It was the last thing he'd been expecting. It wasn't simply the perspicacity ingrained in the query: it was ... What was it? Bingham was unsure. He'd expected the child to offer his name. Children always wanted you to know their names, and yet here was one who was reluctant to give his own but curious about you and your family.

"Yes," he said, "she is part-Italian. Her mother was Italian and her father was English."

"Are they dead now?"

"Yes," replied Bingham, taken aback only by the intelligence implied. To this boy he must seem very old and so his wife would be old, too.

"What is her name?"

"Lina."

"That's a funny name."

At last, a spark!

"I like it," replied Bingham.

"Is it Italian?"

"No, it's ..."

Bingham felt unable to go into a long explanation of how his wife came to be called 'Lina'. He felt this child would quarry him for details of American jazz singers and Italian spelling.

"Her daddy liked the name," he said, "I expect your daddy likes yours ..."

There was hesitation in every line of the boy's body: his hand went to his mouth, his feet curled in his sandals. Bingham leaned forward, tilting his head to one side. The movement wasn't motivated only by his deafness: he wanted to engage the boy, to show he was interested.

"What is your name?" he asked, at last.

The old woman rose to her feet. She had seemed reassured by Bingham's more or less constant translations and even leaned her sloppy bulk forward as though taking an interest in the boy's curiosity, but now she stood decisively. There was no doubt about her stance: she might have been an Amazon guarding her queen, Bingham judged by the flaring of her nostrils and the raising of her forehead. Was her English better than he'd supposed?

"I faut y aller!" she said.

The boy stood at once and the old woman took him by the hand so quickly that the little car was left abandoned. Bingham knelt, retrieved the treasured possession and handed it to the boy."

"If you must go," he said, "don't forget your car."

He inclined his head and smiled at the old woman but there was no response other than the coldness of the command left on the air.

"Au revoir, Madame. Bonne journée."

Whatever happened, he wanted to end on a pleasant note. The old woman smiled. There was hesitation in the smile but none in her reply.

"Au revoir, Monsieur."

The next moment she and the child were gone, mingling with people hurrying to work or possibly the shops, disappearing towards the old town, away from the festival tourists crowding the pavements along La Croisette: tourists who would be gathering to claim their tickets for the previews of the day.

Bingham thought of Lina and checked that his mobile phone was switched on: for some reason, she always felt the need to be able to contact him at a moment's notice. He, then, hurried off in pursuit of the old woman and the boy, eager not to lose them, equally eager not to be seen.

They'd headed towards Rue Meynadier, a thoroughfare of markets and shops – offering fruit, vegetables, meat, groceries and clothes – running parallel to the port. It also held a number of souvenir and cheap gift shops to tempt the tourists, but at that early hour Bingham heard only French voices.

He hurried along, mingling easily with the locals, catching sight, now and then, of the head of the old woman, her hair tied up but with stray strands flopping loosely around her neck and shoulders. She moved clumsily, rocking from side to side in the way of fat people. Bingham imagined her legs, the thighs nudging each other, the feet waddling duck-like in her hurry to be away. She never looked back but pressed on steadily, appearing at last from the row of shops and making a swift turn uphill and to her right.

It was there Bingham lost her. He wasn't sure how. One moment she seemed to be ahead of him, no doubt panting slightly on the slope, and then she was gone. Bingham found himself on a small incline. To his left were the houses of the local people, adorned with tubs, baskets and boxes of bright red flowers and to his right a narrow alleyway leading to further houses and apartments. Bingham realized that he had left the Cannes of the film makers and the tourists and was among the real people of this little, French town.

He felt annoyed but, at the same time, relaxed. Somehow, he knew he'd find the old woman and the little boy who might, or might not, be her grandson, but how or why was beyond him.

If he remembered his last visit correctly, which had been in his youth, so many years ago, he had reached the old town, Le Suquet, which overlooks the west end of the port. Le Suquet is a warren of narrow streets, squares and passageways that climb up and around the hill, with a fine view from the top.

Bingham walked about for a while, searching the alleys, peering down the passageways that separated the houses, houses tightly packed on the hillside. Sweating from his exertions, he eventually returned to the Rue Meynadier, where he'd seen a little café, one among several but one that attracted him. It was elegant in an everyday kind of way with neat tablecloths in gingham, as spotless as a proud homeowner might keep their own kitchen and dining room.

Here, he compounded his mistakes of the day by entering the café and asking for a coffee. He should have known better. The owner, a man with heavy jowls and a bushy, sweating moustache, looked first at his wife and then nodded towards the door, as though ordering Bingham out, and returned, without a word, to polishing the glasses with a crisp tea-towel.

Bingham sat outside, under the striped awning, at one of the immaculately set tables, looking up and down the thoroughfare, and waited.

A very old lady arrived and sat at the table next to him on the further side of the door. Even Bingham - who was tidy, perhaps fastidious, in his appearance – was impressed with how she looked. It could not have been easy, at her age, to present herself to the world so elegantly attired at such a relatively early hour. Her skirt and jacket were jet black and set off by a silk scarf around her neck. The scarf bore a flowered pattern that was predominantly red in colour, the red of geraniums. In her grey hair, not a strand of which was out of place, she wore a neat, little fascinator that matched, perfectly, the black of her outfit and captured the red of her scarf. She looked neither to the left nor right but seemed content to sit quietly, a gentle smile on her face.

The café owner's wife appeared with a tray holding a coffee cup, a tiny jug of cream, a chic cafetiere and a small pastry. Without a word, she placed this on the table in front of the elderly lady, pressed down the plunger and poured the first cup. Not a word was passed between the two women, although a smile may have been exchanged. Bingham wasn't sure: after all, the wife's back was towards him.

The ceremony over, she turned to Bingham.

"Maintenant, Monsieur?"

It was all she said. The café was *now* ready to honour him with its attention and pleased to serve him.

Bingham wasn't sure when the idea came to him. He didn't see how it could have anything to do with the old lady or the excellent cup of coffee and pastry served to him by the patron's wife. It was often so: immersed in one chain of thought, an idea – usually at odds with his preoccupation – suddenly appeared.

When he'd finished, he paid his *l'addition*, remembering to leave the small amount of change, gave the lady a smile with the most discreet of nods and made his way to one of the souvenir and gift shops he'd noticed when failing to shadow, successfully, the little boy and the old woman who might be his grandmother.

Chapter Two
THE PATRONNE

Bingham was back in the old town, Le Suquet. Here, bars, restaurants and cafes rubbed shoulders so closely that it was a wonder they all made a living.

Some, lingering along hidden passages, seemed to cater for their own clientele of regular locals. They were less fussy in appearance but still welcoming. Bingham now remembered he should wait to be served, rather than going straight to the bar where he'd expect a slightly cold shoulder from the patron for his impertinence.

It was lunchtime. Bingham had been here since he'd enjoyed his coffee, asking questions. The little rubber ball he'd bought at the souvenir shop was in his hand. He'd dirtied the ball very slightly to give the appearance that the little boy had bounced and lost it. The ball gave Bingham an excuse for his search, although what he'd do or say when, or if, he found the couple, he had yet to decide.

His query was the same wherever he went: café, bar, garage. He was looking for a little, English boy who is holidaying with his grandmother. Bingham's French – honed from his grammar school education by the travels of his youth – was more than adequate: some of those he asked even considered him to be a local or, at least, French.

This was good because the French loath hearing their language spoken in an ugly fashion even if they turn a blind eye to their own pronunciation of English. Indeed, Bingham had found them unforgiving of foreigners and had often been answered in very bad English – almost, he thought, as a reprisal – when he first visited their country and tried to make himself understood.

Bingham didn't share the English aversion to the French. He liked them. It was characteristic of the man that he recognised the beauty of difference; and they were different – their culture, their language, their moral outlook.

But no one seemed willing to help, even those who accepted him as one of their own.

"I don't know anything. I've nothing to hide," replied the woman at the first café, "I've never seen the old lady."

"I know she passed this way."

"She didn't stop here."

"She was going home, I expect."

The woman shrugged.

"Perhaps the little boy was tired."

Again, the shrug: the shoulders not only up and down but in a dismissive movement.

"You've no idea where she might have gone?"

"Why should I?"

"She was a local person. She would have passed this way many times."

"Many people pass this way. I cannot be expected to know them all."

"A fat, old lady with a beautiful child: I think you would have noticed her."

"I have a café to run, Monsieur. Please excuse me."

Bingham walked on deeper into the labyrinths of the old town. Truth to tell, he was beginning to enjoy himself. He'd asked questions before but never in quite this way: never by endlessly treading the pavements eliminating one possibility after another. Always, his questions had led him on to a query if not an answer.

His old policeman friend, Simon Brockie, would laugh if he could see Bingham at this moment. Real police work, he would say: wearing out the shoe leather to no avail, asking questions that had to be asked.

Bingham's second port of call had been a garage, much to his surprise. What was a garage doing in this charming, if rough, area? The mechanic, wiping his hands slowly on an oily rag, looked Bingham up and down before shrugging.

The attitude annoyed Bingham and he stared the man out, waiting for an answer. The man's shoulders were high, his exhaled breathe long. The mechanic was anxious, despite his nonchalant pose. He hadn't yet made up his mind. Was Bingham more or less than he seemed? He was dressed smartly enough to be a copper, but his demeanour suggested nothing more than a tourist, unnaturally concerned about something trivial.

"You've seen them pass? Spare me the need to return. Which way did they go?"

The man, adjusting his cigarette to the corner of his mouth, a gesture that reminded Bingham of those 1960s French film stars, jerked his head in the opposite direction to which Bingham had come.

"You saw them go that way? I don't want to waste my time."

The mechanic nodded, this time with a look that might have been intended to suggest sincerity.

"You'll be here if I have to return?" said Bingham, injecting a tone of what he hoped was menace in his voice.

The man nodded again, and Bingham made his way deeper into the rambling passageways of the old town. He was looking for a home, somewhere a grandmother could look after the child in her care. It wouldn't be luxurious and it wouldn't be tidy, but it would be homely, a place where a child could play and nod off to sleep when he was tired. Would there be flowers on the doorstep? Bingham wasn't sure. He thought the old lady too lazy to bother with decoration.

And he wouldn't be pursuing them if he didn't have doubts, would he? Was she the boy's grandmother, and if she wasn't, what was her business with the child? He thought back to his first impressions. They had been at odds with each other, uncomfortable in each other's company. Bingham was sure of his feelings. They didn't look as though they belonged together: that had been his first reaction, and it was the reason he was walking through a French town with a rubber ball in his hands, asking questions.

It was at the ninth, or perhaps the tenth, café where he struck almost lucky. He gained no more in the way of information, but he experienced what the French called a *frisson*, an apprehension.

He had turned from one alleyway into another and then another until he felt quite lost. He wasn't troubled. Here was the real world of this little town, the world that existed before and after the famous film festival. Looking up he could see women hanging out their washing, line after line of sheets stretched across the passages.

There were two bars that attracted his attention and he walked into the one that looked cleaner. At the counter he said, simply:

"Une biere."

He'd learned long ago that it didn't do to be too courteous to French waiters or bartenders. It was more than likely to be taken as condescending, rather a lack of respect than politeness. In France, waiting on table was a noble profession: the waiter and the customer were on an equal footing. No overt courtesy was needed and nor was it necessary to name the beer: the waiter would know.

Bingham sat quietly, sipping the light drink, waiting for the bartender, should he wish, to start a conversation. Bingham placed the red, rubber ball on the counter and glanced at it, idly. As far as the bartender, who was probably the patron, was concerned, the ball might hold the secrets of the universe.

He wiped the counter, lifting the ball in the process and smiling at Bingham with raised eyebrows.

"A child's toy," said Bingham, feigning tiredness in his voice, "He was with his grandmother and he left his ball in the grass. I thought I might take a walk and find them, but ..." and he shrugged and raised his shoulders in a gesture of resignation.

"A boy of four or five? The woman fat?"

"Yes."

The bartender nodded across the narrow street. Bingham drained off his glass, placed slightly more than enough euros on the counter, smiled and walked to the other bar.

It was not a prepossessing place: in short, it was grubby. He was reminded of a pub in his wife's native county, Suffolk, where the bar measured no more than fifteen feet by seven; but whereas the pub in Bury St Edmunds was pristine in its cleanliness and where the woodwork and brasses were polished to a high shine, this bar looked as though it hadn't seen a duster, let alone a tin of polish, for years.

There was a narrow counter on which a few glasses stood idle and a small wooden table with two armless chairs. At the far end was what appeared to be a doorway; this was separated from the bar by a curtain of wooden beads. The curtain had been hung carelessly from a strip of plastic-covered wire.

Bingham knew there were a number of people beyond the curtain because voices stopped talking when he entered, but he couldn't make out how many or who they might be. There was very little light in the bar and none percolated through to illuminate the room behind the beads.

Bingham sensed a certain antagonism towards his presence and so he leaned on the counter and tapped with a one-euro piece.

The woman who pushed her way through the curtain was wrinkled. In an attempt to hide this sign of age she had covered her face with make-up, but not very successfully and the only effect was to make her look older.

"Monsieur?"

The tone was polite enough but the tautness of her body and the way she made no attempt to approach Bingham suggested that she wanted him out on the street.

"Une biere, s'il vous plait."

He wasn't sure why this time he'd added the note of courtesy, and then realised it was because he was talking to a woman.

"We have nothing on tap."

"A bottle will do, Madame. I've been walking all morning and I am thirsty."

"You are here for the festival?"

"Yes and no. My wife is here for the festival. I am here because my wife is here."

In England, this remark would have gained him a smile, if not a laugh and possibly a retort, but the woman's face did not so much as crease. It was a comment gently laced with the humour of what the papers call the battle of the sexes; but in France, Bingham knew that sex was not a laughing matter.

She brought the beer round and placed it on the table, standing a glass beside it and indicating that Bingham might sit down. He realised that she was moving him as far as possible from the room beyond the curtain, from where all conversation had ceased.

Bingham poured the beer and noticed that the glass was clean to the point of shining, and this surprised him, given the general appearance of the bar. Noticing the woman about to make her way back, Bingham decided to engage her in conversation.

"At home, we have a bar very similar to yours. It is called The Nutshell," he said, adding, "because of its size."

The woman turned, marginally, a natural courtesy overcoming, however slightly, her desire to be rid of this man. She nodded a smile but said nothing.

"I see your place is called Le Canape. Do you serve food?"

The woman smiled as though of a memory long ago.

"What would Monsieur like? We have a leg of lamb."

"I don't eat meat," replied Bingham, "Some cheese perhaps?"

Another slight smile followed. Bingham wondered whether this was at his dislike of meat or whether the woman was thinking of what she might prepare.

There was some murmuring from beyond the curtain and the sound of cutlery clattering on plates; the woman's friends had relaxed, stopped listening and were tucking into the mutton, but the voices were too low for Bingham to hear what was said.

A few minutes after she'd disappeared, the woman emerged with an open sandwich on a plate: avocado and goat's cheese on a very lightly toasted baguette.

"Another beer, Monsieur?"

Bingham nodded. He wasn't fond of avocado, considering it rather tasteless, but underlying the strong goat's cheese it provided a delicious lunch, and the baguette, which might have been served just as it came from the bakery, was untroubled by the light toasting. There was pride in this grubby little bar and Bingham was curious.

"I spent some time in France," he said, "when I was a young man, but this is the first time I have stayed in Cannes. This morning I sat outside the Potiniere and watched the world go by. It's delightful."

"Your wife is with you, Monsieur?"

"With a friend, attending one of the many films you show. I chose to wander. I like the old places in a town. I feel at home in your bar."

There was something about the woman that did not add up. Her look suggested an old tart, but her manner, a housewife. He'd noticed the smile when he mentioned the name of the bar: Le Canape – an open sandwich or a sofa.

As a young man – in particular, a young Englishman of a straight, if not exactly strict, upbringing – he'd been bewildered, if not shocked, by the French attitude to sex. It didn't carry the same opprobrium as it did in England. It seemed to him that the French saw the enjoyment of sex as a right rather than a privilege; this applied to women as much as men, as he'd discovered quite alarmingly one day. There was no sense in which sex and sin were linked in the public mind.

He wasn't sure why these thoughts were going through his head at that moment, other than that there were in some way, yet to be defined, connected with the woman.

"Madame Couchet?" he asked, attempting, yet again, to draw her into conversation.

"Yes, Monsieur."

"I saw the name on the licence plate. This is your bar?"

"My husband's … many years ago. When he died, I carried on with the business. It provides me with an income – enough to get me by."

"You cater for the locals?

"And people like yourself who wander in from the festival or the seafront … whenever."

She seemed friendly enough, despite Bingham's initial feelings that she bore some hostility towards him. Perhaps he had disturbed her lunch with friends?

Still, there was some reason why he did not ask, directly, the question he needed answering. If he'd understood the barman's nod correctly, the fat woman and the child must have come into La Canape. Where were they now?

The beers had gone to his head. He'd had three in the space of what turned out to be his lunch hour, and he couldn't remember how many others at the bars he'd visited. They were only those little bottles of French beer, of course, but he couldn't drink as much as when he was a young man. Bingham felt his eyes flicker and knew he needed to sleep.

"You are tired, Monsieur?"

"I'm afraid so."

"You may nod off here if you wish. You will not be disturbed. Not at this hour."

"Won't your friends find it odd – a stranger asleep in the bar?"

"We're all friends here, Monsieur."

"My name's George, George Bingham."

He held out his hand and the woman took it. Hers was dry and crisp like paper left out in the sun.

"Isabelle Couchet."

"I'm pleased to meet you."

Isabelle Couchet turned away and disappeared for the second time through the curtain. There was a murmur of voices, some quiet laughter, followed by the sound of eating. Bingham dozed. He might have been at home.

When he woke it was to the clatter of plates being placed in a sink. He wasn't sure how long he'd slept but felt it couldn't have been for many minutes. He walked to the curtain and pulled it aside, something he'd wanted to do since he arrived.

Isabelle was standing at the sink. Sitting round a table that was no larger than the one in the bar were three people: a young woman dressed up to the nines, an old man who looked as though he might have only recently emerged from his bed and a very smart sailor of the weekend variety. The girl and the old man were clearly locals but the sailor seemed to be a foreigner.

"Excuse me," said Bingham, "I'd no wish to intrude. How long have I been asleep?"

"Twenty minutes, Monsieur, no more. Are you in a hurry?"

"No, I've all afternoon."

"Another beer?" asked Isabelle Couchet.

The others round the table laughed.

"Perhaps a coffee would be more to the purpose," replied Bingham, smiling.

"Won't you sit down?"

"You find our beer too strong for your taste, Monsieur?" said the old man, digging the sailor in the ribs.

"I've had a few this morning as I walked from cafe to bar ... and to garage," replied Bingham, not one to be put down and yet not wanting to rise to the bait.

"You are *doing the rounds*, hmm?" suggested the sailor, emphasising the English phrase and proud of his ability to speak the language.

Bingham seized his chance: he was fairly sure that the others round the table had only, at the best, a rough grasp of English.

"I've been looking for a young boy – four or five years old – who was on the seafront this morning. He was with a lady who might have been his grandmother. I was told he'd come in here. This is his ball."

"Came and went," replied the sailor, "They were here five minutes at the most. Gave Isabelle a hug and a kiss, collected some pastries from her and *Bob's your uncle*!"

The sailor looked up at Isabelle who'd listened to the exchange, a frown creasing her already wrinkled forehead further, and explained what Bingham had said.

"Why did you not mention this before, Monsieur?"

Bingham couldn't say what he actually thought, of course: that he had this feeling things were not quite right, that he would not have been told the truth.

"I felt I might be intruding on a private matter," he said.

Isabelle looked at the sailor who shrank back from the anger in her eyes.

"What have you said?" she asked him.

"That your friends were here briefly and left. Is there a problem?"

"There might be. Who are you?" she asked, turning to Bingham.

"A tourist – no more. I spoke with the little boy and … and wanted to return his ball."

"I think it best if you leave now Monsieur."

"If you know the boy and his grandmother perhaps you would tell them that I have the ball?"

"You may leave it here."

"I'd like to say hello again," replied Bingham, "I am staying at the Majestic Hotel. It's on the …"

"I know where it is, Monsieur," replied Isabelle, indicting by her tone that she also knew it was the kind of place where you might pay twenty-five euros for a gin and tonic.

Bingham stepped back, brushing against the bead curtain. The sailor looked troubled rather than angry but the eyes of the old man and the young girl were hostile. Isabelle Couchet looked as though she had been deceived, betrayed and – perhaps, worst of all – made to look foolish.

Bingham felt he'd been deceitful but in a good cause. Holding back with his query had gained him confirmation that the old woman and the boy had been here, among friends, and that these people had something to hide.

He'd reached the outside door and was passing into the street when Isabelle's voice called to him.

"Who are you?"

"I told you the truth. There was no deceit in what I said. I am here with my wife for the festival."

"You are not a detective?"

"No."

Isabelle Couchet closed the door behind him and turned the welcome sign to *Ferme*. It was clear she did not believe him.

Chapter Three
THE OLD MAN

Bingham walked away from La Canape but only as far as the corner of a nearby alley, and there he waited. His one attempt to shadow a suspect, two years before, had been notably unsuccessful but he lived in hope.

Isabelle would be a poor bet: she'd be on the alert. He didn't fancy following the girl: if she noticed, he might look like – or even be accused of being – a dirty old man. The sailor would, presumably, lead him back to one of the luxury boats that loafed around in the marina, and he didn't think that the boy and the old woman were part of that set; and so he was left with the old man.

Bingham had seen him only briefly but reckoned him to be crusty: awkward, unhelpful, belligerent – at the best, surly. But he was a likely lead: it didn't seem possible that he knew nothing of the pair Bingham sought.

While waiting, he suddenly realised that he'd forgotten to phone Lina and had committed the crime of crimes by switching off his mobile phone when he was in the bar. He remedied his deficiency as a husband by switching the phone back on. Lina's was on voicemail. She was probably enjoying the lunch he'd missed and hadn't really wanted to attend. He was sure

Patrizio would keep her entertained with more tales of himself. Bingham left an apology saying he'd explain later and switched off.

It was a warm afternoon. The heat was climbing to its zenith and even in the shade Bingham began to sweat. The sun, its brilliance obscuring the blue of the sky, seemed to seek him out wherever he moved. At that point in the day, the sun peered down into every alleyway.

He looked back at the doorway of Couchet's bar, wondering who the man might have been and what he did for a living. Bingham had the feeling that running the bar wasn't the full extent of his business: Isabelle's half-smiles suggested as much.

He tried to picture what they might be doing. He knew French lunches were an extended affair and was sobered by the thought that they might sleep it off in Isabelle's galley. People passed, looked him up and down and walked on. It was very hot and very quiet: siesta time. His brief doze hadn't rested him and Bingham was almost tempted to cross to the other bar, where the patron had been helpful, order a drink and sleep on it.

He'd considered this at least three or four times, when the sailor appeared and walked off in the direction of the harbour without looking round. He was followed by the young woman who crossed the passageway and disappeared along a side alley, and then by the old man who came towards Bingham in a slow, shuffling motion.

Bingham had time to take him in before stepping back into a small passage between the houses. Surly, certainly, and burly: the old man looked as though he might have been a boxer in his younger days. His hands were large and his nose was bulbous and broken. The face was puffed up, so much so that the eyes were hidden in the flesh of the cheeks. This appearance of drunkenness was enhanced by the drooping mouth and the heavy jowls.

He wore a white jacket that might have been bought in his youth when the muscles were firmer, and would have been a relaxed fit: now, it gripped him tightly across the shoulders and fell short of his wrists. The old man was clearly used to the heat because he wore a cardigan under the jacket. This was unbuttoned most of the way and hung loosely over his trousers, held out by a pot belly.

He passed by Bingham without a glance and stumbled his way along the paving slabs. His shoulders hung forward and his arms swung at his sides so that his progress seemed similar to that of a chimpanzee. Bingham fell in behind, not worried the old man might turn because it occurred to him that the effort would have been too great.

Bingham saw his own weariness reflected in the other's walk. He was conscious that his mind was back in La Canape while his body was entering another world: a place of closed passageways, overhead linen lines, hidden chatter emerging from open windows and the soft sibilance of an afternoon's rest.

He began to paint for himself a picture of the daily life of this place, of the old man's routine. Did he go to Couchet's regularly? Bingham thought so, and the young woman as well, but as friends rather than family. Was it usually for lunch or with some other purpose in mind? They would chat, no doubt, especially the old couple.

Time placed no pressure on them, but what about the young woman? He knew that work for its own sake was held in low esteem in France. There was no

Protestant work ethic here: work was simply a means to an end. He'd wondered, as a young man facing up to forty years as a teacher, how the people he met earned their money, but never arrived at an answer. Extended lunch hours, quite novel even now at home, were routine in the France he remembered.

In his rather puritanical way, Bingham hadn't approved of this morality; he'd never moved beyond seeing it as laziness. He readily accepted the notion of cultural differences but surely the enjoyment of work was a virtue in itself, wasn't it?

He'd once asked the question 'why?' – a habit he'd kept all his life – but received only uncomprehending smiles in reply or nods that said simply 'the English!'. Later, when the truth began to emerge and Bingham faced a decision of his own, he was to reflect on his thoughts as he followed the old man, thoughts linked, as always, to a sense of place.

They came after what seemed ages so slow was their progress – although it can have been for no longer than five or ten minutes – to a courtyard onto which opened a number of doors and stairways.

Bingham was familiar with such places and loved them. Throughout those countries that bordered the Mediterranean these little courtyards – the meeting places of neighbours all of whom had to pass through them at some time during the day – were common. They taunted the English love of privacy, where neighbours might be almost complete strangers.

He watched the old man climb one of the stone stairways and disappear through the door at the top. Bingham looked around him. It was a rough-looking courtyard – the paving slabs broken in places, the stairways without rails and uneven, odd pieces of furniture and a child's toy or two left at the foot of the stairs, a makeshift line propped up – but beautified by the pots and tubs of flowers, geraniums mainly, that decorated each doorway and the steps leading to them.

Bingham was considering his next move when a window above opened and a head peered out. It was the old man and he had a cigarette in his hand. He was looking across the rooftops and had not noticed Bingham. It is strange how impressions received unconsciously at the time, are remembered later. Bingham realised that the bar hadn't smelled of smoke: musty, yes, and dusty, but no smoke. The old man had come home for a cigarette and seemed obliged to enjoy it leaning from his window.

He flicked the ash from the end and caught sight of Bingham. He stared for a while, the strain of not knowing twisting his face into angry shapes. Eventually, he said, apology in every syllable:

"Monsieur, I know you, don't I?"

"We have met," replied Bingham.

"I have your name in my head, but I can't, I …"

He tapped his head, which Bingham noticed for the first time was bald. There were tears of frustration in the old man's eyes.

"It's here, you see … that's what's wrong. I'll come down."

Once seated on the steps, he offered Bingham a cigarette. Although he didn't smoke, Bingham accepted the offer – it seemed politic – and drew in a mouthful of tobacco.

"I had the trouble, you know, and so I don't remember."

"My name's Bingham, George Bingham."

"No, no, I haven't got that ... Were we boys together? I knew your father. Yes, I remember him. He was a devil. He gave your mother the run-around. Never knew where he was. Lost so much money at the casino, he couldn't go home. Daren't go home! He liked my company, but I didn't have the money to spare ..."

The old man's voice wandered off in time with his memory. It had all gone again. Bingham could see him grasping at wisps in the wind.

"We talked of the boy," said Bingham, "He would be four or five."

"No, no. I had two girls, no boys. They're long gone. She wasn't right, you see – not right in the head – their mother. You can't talk to her. She sits there, rocking ..."

Again, Bingham watched those awful tears spring into the eyes. Was the wife alive? Was she up there, now, rocking backwards and forwards in a chair or was the old man's memory an old one, one long gone?

"You enjoy the company at Couchet's?"

"You were with Jehane! I remember. She was a good woman. How do you find her?"

"She seems very pleasant. I was wondering about the boy."

"He went off, but it's all right now. She worries too much, but he'll be fine ... It's the women, see – they muddle a man. I squared up to him, you know. I wasn't having any of that nonsense ... I was a boxer in the army. My opponent was a fine-looking man ... lovely shape to him, and he could throw a punch, put the weight of his body behind it, but I'm a bruiser and I took it. I can take punishment. On the chest it was, but I took it. You've got to be able to take a punch ... I can still throw one, you know."

Bingham was sure he could, if only he'd be able to remember why he was fighting.

"Have you known Madame Couchet long?"

"Isabelle is a jewel among women, an angel sent from God … It wasn't right … I squared up to him. I can throw a punch."

"She is a kind woman – kind to the young girl, kind to Jehane."

Bingham tried to remove the questioning from his tone, making his comments sound more like agreements.

"You know her?" asked the old man.

"Jehane?"

"She wasn't right for him. He came home. I'm not saying it's right, but that's life."

"And the little boy?" asked Bingham, eager to pin down the old man's memories.

"He ran off."

"When was this?"

"He was young, but that's what they do. He came back again."

"Masson, Masson!" called a voice from above.

Bingham looked up at the old man's open window. It must be his wife calling, but Bingham couldn't let him go – not yet, not until the bits and pieces of his reminiscences made sense.

He needn't have worried. The old man spat on the ground – a gesture of contempt.

"Masson, Masson!" he mimicked, "Always Masson, Masson! She isn't right in the head."

"Your wife?"

"Madame Paquet! She was proud of that name once. When we married, I was cock of the heap …"

It wasn't an expression Bingham had ever come across, but he managed to picture a cockerel crowing on top of a dung hill. At least he had a name: Masson Paquet must be the old man. Was it the grandmother in the room? Had he found the boy?

"He took up with another woman, you see, but that was afterwards."

"Your son?"

"I didn't have a son – you know that my friend. Two daughters – you remember?"

"Of course! The little boy? He ...?"

Bingham left the question hanging hopefully.

"I knew him then but he is above me now. Had him on my lap bouncing him and down, but they grow up and go away. There's nothing you can do but help them when they need you ... "

"Children are all the same," said Bingham, not believing a word he said but hoping it might encourage Masson Paquet to speak further.

"She is unhappy, but things will change. Rome wasn't built in a day."

"Women are always hoping for things to get better – hmm?"

"She is a goddess ... We sit and talk, nothing more."

"She helps the boy?"

Masson nodded, but Bingham was unsure whether it was a nod for now or for a memory. There were two boys somewhere in the old man's mind.

"I squared up to him."

"He treated her badly?"

"An angel sent from God."

"Masson, Masson!"

The voice was shriller as it called a second time.

"A moment, Simone, one moment! I am speaking with Jean. Have you a cigarette?"

"I'm sorry," said Bingham, "I've run out. I was on my way to get some when …"

"Not round here. You'll need to go back. Where was it we met?"

"At Isabelle's."

"You came in. I remember you. I saw you look round the curtain. You're not Jean."

"George, George Bingham. I'm looking for the little boy and … and his grandmother."

"You won't find them here. What are you doing here?"

Masson Paquet's tone had changed suddenly; the rambling old man became a suspicious one.

Bingham took the ball from his pocket and tossed it in the air.

"You remember now?"

"She's an angel among women."

"Isabelle?"

"Masson, Masson!"

"I'm coming."

The old man looked Bingham squarely in the eye, as once he must have sized up an opponent. Bingham stood slowly and held out the ball.

"If you see the boy, please give him this from the man on the Croisette."

Bingham wasn't sure why he handed over the ball, but this was often the case with him: intuition prevailed. Was it anticipation that Masson Paquet might help or simply to sidestep a possible thump? He wasn't sure.

"I'll call in tomorrow," he said, "Tell Isabelle to expect me."

He stepped back and walked from the courtyard, turning to wave at the other man when he reached the passageway. Masson Paquet was still sitting on the third step, his feet resting on the first, holding the red ball in his free hand and staring into space as he searched back in his memory.

*

It was still only late afternoon rather than early evening and Bingham wondered what to do. Buy some cigarettes in case he and Masson met up again? Yes, he'd shop for a smoke because the old man would remember that it was he who had offered the last one.

Wander down to the marina and try to find the sailor? Perhaps, but what would he know?

Sit quietly somewhere and try to sort out the names in his head? Yes, that would be best. He'd talk it through. Who was Jehane? Was Simone the grandmother? And the two boys – how were they related, or were they one and the same person? 'He took up with another woman … but that was afterwards'. After what? Who was Masson talking about: Couchet or another man? It seemed to be Couchet to whom he'd squared up, but Bingham wasn't absolutely sure. And there was someone, he'd bounced up and down on his lap. But when – yesterday or decades ago?

As he meditated, he walked and soon found himself in Rue Meynadier and outside the little café where he'd annoyed the patron earlier. Bingham sat down and waited. The wife arrived after a while and smiled; the Englishman was learning their ways. He smiled back and she returned with a coffee and a pastry. It was freshly baked. A man given to tea at teatime and coffee at coffee time, he enjoyed the change and celebrated the difference. Anyway, the French couldn't make tea to save their lives, but then making coffee the way they did – the best coffee in the world – they didn't have to make a decent brew.

It was here, sitting in this exact spot, on the same chair, under this very striped awning, admiring the neat gingham tablecloth and the immaculately set table, the idea of the red ball had come to him; and it was here that Bingham now thought of Brockie.

Once a copper, always a copper; his old friend, Simon Brockie had never lost the habit of following the latest crime, especially if it involved missing children. It was a missing child he'd failed to find that had haunted him through to his retirement: Natalie Beddoes, who had been the subject of Bingham's first search. He'd phone Brockie. Once he had a name, should a name emerge, life would be so much easier.

Chapter Four
THE SAILOR

"Do you fancy a walk into the old town, tonight, Lina?" asked Bingham, when they met up back at their hotel.

"You know we can't, Bing."

"Why?"

"Patrizio has asked us out for a drink."

"Ah."

"Is the walk important?"

"Hmm! No, no. We've said we'll go for a drink … and we must. Sorry about lunch. I fell asleep."

Lina laughed, walked across their hotel room and put her arms around her husband.

"Tell me about your day. You've heard about mine."

It was true. They'd met on the harbour wall as planned and Bingham had listened patiently while his wife relayed the details of her day with her old lover. Patrizio had been charming, as Bingham expected, and they'd enjoyed "an enviable lunch" at L'Assiette Provencale. The filet de Durande had been "cooked to perfection", the tarte citron meringue was "out of this world" and the whole experience had been "topped off" with a glass of verre vin rose.

"What did you do in the afternoon?" asked Bingham.

"Patrizio walked me along the Croisette and introduced me to one or two of his friends. He's dying to get to know you, Bing."

"I can't wait to further our acquaintance," was Bingham's reply.

"And you?" asked Lina, laughing.

"I'll tell you when we get up to our room."

And he did, not forgetting to mention the open sandwich of avocado and goat's cheese on a lightly toasted baguette.

"Don't you think you may have over-reacted, Bing?"

"You mean to the goat's cheese …"

"No."

"It's the lack of intimacy between the old woman and the boy and Isabelle's asking whether I was a detective – oh, and the hostility I felt in the bar – oh, and the fact she threw me out after I'd quizzed the sailor – that disturbs me."

"If you feel strongly, perhaps you'd better contact the police."

"Contacting the police in France isn't like walking into a police station at home and having a chat with your friendly neighbourhood bobby, Lina."

"We don't have friendly neighbourhood bobbies, anymore, Bing."

"The principle remains, if not the practice; in France, whether to pursue an investigation or not rests with the local magistrate. He – and, I suppose, she, these days – leads the investigation. Only the evidence considered by the magistrate counts in court. Magistrates come from a long line of magistrates – they stretch back generations – and they are never wrong – you understand? Fallibility doesn't enter into the matter, and my feelings do not amount to evidence. They'd wave me aside as soon as look at me."

"You're going to pursue this, aren't you?"

"Yes, and that's why I wondered whether we might take a walk into the old town tonight, but never mind – tomorrow will do."

"You do know it's Patrizio's film tomorrow, don't you?"

"And I'm invited?"

"You know you are. We get our tickets in the morning."

"You have yours already, perhaps mine will …"

"No, Bing, I have the accreditation badge already but …"

"And the goody bag."

"And the goody bag, but we have to queue for the tickets."

"A French queue?"

"A French queue. Patrizio is keen for you to come, Bing."

"I'll be there. In the meantime, let's get ready for this evening."

"Have you contacted Brockie?"

"Yes. I don't think the boy's been in France long. You know how quickly children pick up another language? Well, he wasn't comfortable with French but was quite chatty in English."

"Do you think it's a kidnap?"

"I don't think anything at the moment, Lina. I simply live in hope."

*

Bingham quite enjoyed dressing up. He'd done a bit of acting in various Norwich theatres since his retirement and a dinner jacket was simply another costume to him. Like many men of his generation, he took the line that whatever he wore was simply to enhance his wife's appearance. Lina chose a black dress trimmed with silver at the neck, and so Bingham went for his regular dinner jacket, knotting the bow tie for himself, a technique he'd learned from a Budweiser beer mat his eldest son put his way.

"The inconspicuous escort," he said, with a chuckle, having told Lina she looked "great".

"You'd look more Cannes in your white jacket, Bing."

"If you say so," he replied and changed immediately to the one he'd really wanted to wear.

Bingham actually liked Patrizio. Envy was absent from his range of emotions and what Lina might have got up to in her youth was, he considered, none of his business. Besides, he liked characters, and Patrizio Lucatti was certainly one of those. He had a certain camp quality, something Bingham had noticed in heterosexual men who'd spent time in the theatrical world. In a gay man, the quality seemed natural; in one who was straight, Bingham assumed it to be an affectation. To someone as naturally quiet as Bingham, anyone affected was welcome because they always did the talking and rarely listened to others; to Bingham, whose hearing loss verged on the severe, it was a relief to be able to listen casually rather than with the usual intense concentration he found necessary.

"Bing!" said Patrizio, taking Bingham's hand and shaking it, before throwing his own arms akimbo, spreading his fingers and talking to anyone who might listen, when they met in the foyer bar of the Majestic.

"George," replied Bingham, "My mother always insisted that people called me by my "proper name", as she put it. She made an exception for Lina, but if she was with us now, she'd be so pleased to hear you call me George."

Bingham's grin as he spoke, the soft tone of his voice and the reference to his mother, robbed his little homily of any offence he might otherwise have caused. Even Lina, who knew what her husband had said to be nonsense, smiled.

"My mother – always the mother with us men," replied Patrizio, embracing Lina and speaking to Bingham at the same time.

"Lina tells me you had a good time today," said Bingham.

Patrizio favoured them again with his expansive gesture as he showed the way to a table on which Bingham observed a reserved sign. The bar was thronged with guests, and Bingham felt embarrassed at being privileged.

"I thought we must get to know each other, George. You will come tomorrow for my Puccini."

"I'm looking forward to it, Patrizio, although he's a little exuberant for my taste. I'm more of a Britten fan."

Patrizio frowned, gasped and held open his arms in an appeal to Lina.

"He's teasing you, Patrizio. Bing is very fond of Puccini."

"Benjamin Britten is so cold, so ... so ascetic."

"Where I come from, Patrizio, our emotions are not always on the surface. They simmer unnoticed but they simmer, nevertheless. Britten's music offers us a reflection of our inner state."

"To simmer unnoticed is not good. If Billy Budd could but have expressed how he felt, he would not have struck and killed his abuser. The words give release to our feelings and Puccini's music offers us that ... expansion."

Lina laughed, feeling like an adolescent again, as the two men fought over her with words.

The evening passed in such a vein with the swapping of stories from the operas, praise for Lina's "special qualities as a singer ... a loss to the world of opera", "a gift to the world of motherhood".

Later, as he tried to sleep, it was to that moment Bingham was recalled: the moment when the director of operas had commented on Billy Budd's inability to express himself, afflicted as he was by his stutter.

*

The next morning, he supposed himself to have little chance. It was the Puccini film and they were to queue, French-style, behind the accreditation badges worn by Lina and Patrizio, for their 'invitation', the word of choice for 'ticket'. Bingham was unsure which of the three badges they possessed; it wouldn't be the Press Badge, of course, but either the Festival Badge or the Marche Badge seemed possible, depending on how important Cannes perceived Patrizio to be. Since he liked the man, Bingham hoped it would be the Marche Badge.

The queues heaved anticipation and excitement, melded together with various aromas including several different kinds of sweat and, worse still, make-up over sweat. Young women stood in the road holding placards asking for anyone who wished to donate them an invitation: some offered to pay, while others seemed to consider it a privilege for the invitation holder to hand one over to them.

Security guards were everywhere but did nothing to stem the flow of people who eased themselves in through the barriers rather than join the end of the queue. Despite disliking queue jumpers, Bingham had some sympathy for the intruders: it was more or less impossible to know where the end of the queue might be, since people came and went, joining the on-going stream at different points.

In his youth, Bingham had learnt something about what the English call 'French rudeness'. The chief weapon against it was to show no courtesy: courtesy being perceived as weakness. If someone decided to shove through the barrier in front of his wife, Bingham stopped them in no uncertain manner, using his elbows and feet. If eye contact was made with the offender, one of two things happened: men assumed a nonchalance, women an air of bonhomie. Both these reactions were feigned, but they covered both the rudeness and the intruder's embarrassment at being confronted; no one appeared to lose face.

In this way, they reached the head of the queue for *Puccini: A Lust for Life* and met the security guard. Patrizio explained the situation in French as faultless as any foreigners can ever be, while the guard watched him with a detached indifference that would have infuriated even the mild-mannered Bingham. When the Italian director had finished, the guard simply said:

"Non, ce n'est pas possible."

"Sono Patrizio Lucatti, direttore consulente di *Puccini: Una Brama di Vita*. Questi sono i miei amici."

The guard merely shrugged, a gesture designed to be annoying and to assert his manhood. Behind them the queue became disgruntled. Bingham looked at Lina and she indicated in the way only a wife can that he was not to intervene.

The row continued and Bingham, on the quiet, enjoyed it. Patrizio had reverted to his own language, either to find the choicest words or to confuse the guard, but the man seemed in no way admonished. After all, as a Frenchman it was not his business to understand the language of foreigners. The crux of the row was that the guard could not permit Bingham to go further but would allow Patrizio and Lina to do so.

Eventually, the queue joined in; a blend of locals and foreigners, it offered support to both sides, but impatience was certainly on the side of the guard, and it was Lina who finally resolved the situation. She whispered something Bingham didn't catch into Patrizio's ear and then addressed the guard in French.

"If that's the way your kind of man treats a guest to your country, then your manhood leaves a lot to be desired. My husband has better things to do this morning than listen to a rooster singing from his dunghill."

She then turned to Bingham and kissed him full on the mouth, something she had never done before in public, to a roar of approval from the crowd and the chagrin of the guard. Her reference to the man's lack of manhood and her comparing him to a cockerel on a dunghill amused Bingham and delighted the crowd. When he kissed Lina farewell and shook Patrizio's hand, he received a round of applause as he slipped away through the barrier.

*

This free time was unexpected, but he hadn't long because they'd been invited to what amounted to a late lunch aboard the *La Fanciulla del West*, a yacht that belonged to one of the film's backers. Besides, Bingham was tired. He found, these days, that he stayed energetic when he focussed on one thing at a time: the morning had been devoted to queueing for the film that was to be screened at the Theatre Croisette at noon and standing had wearied him. A coffee called and so he made his way to the little café on the Rue Meynadier where he'd offended the patron.

This time, he sat and waited, and the café noir and pâtisserie du jour appeared on the gingham cloth without his asking. He smiled at the patron's wife and received a smile back. At the table on the other side of the door sat the elderly lady immaculately attired.

He sat there for almost an hour, feeling guilty at not pursuing his investigation but aware that his knees ached and that all he really wanted to do was rest. Growing old was a joyful experience in many ways, but also a chastening one: a person became aware of limitations they'd overcome without a single thought when younger.

Eventually, his conscience overcame his tiredness and Bingham made his way to the harbour and the marina, where he found himself among the people of Cannes.

The glitz was visible in the limousines, in the hotels and on the beaches but it wasn't overbearing. The ordinary people carried on their lives regardless, enjoying the spectacle and the occasion without being overcome by it; film producers, starlets, tourists and other exotic people may come and go, but the daily baguette needed collecting and the daily dejeuner needed preparing, nonetheless. They walked their many dogs and gazed at yachts, so enormous they might have been liners, knowing full well that the real boats would still be on the blue water when the festival had faded for another year.

He wanted names to conjure with and when he found the sailor he would ask the questions he needed answered. Bingham was convinced that the man, who had seemed willing to talk, worked on one of the visiting boats. Did he live here in Cannes, offering his services along the harbour or was he an annual visitor? Of one thing Bingham was certain: the man was Dutch. Bingham had guessed that fact from his accent. How many Dutchmen came ashore in Cannes during the festival?

*

It was at the late lunch aboard *La Fanciulla del West* that this question was answered. Patrizio was only too pleased to ask the owner of the yacht and the owner only too pleased to ask the captain who was only too pleased to enquire among the crew.

Bingham's description of the sailor – short, wiry, blond, sharply dressed, with a twist to his smile and the ability to speak at least three languages – brought him a name: Tage Lauwers. It brought a name and a ribald laugh when he spoke to the crew member who was summoned to speak with him. Tage Lauwers was a lady's man who enjoyed the company of "all sorts". This was well-known among the crew. Tage wasn't fussy and he would provide introductions on request.

"He is a local, then?" asked Bingham.

"He lives here, making his living along the waterfront, and he always offers his services when the festival comes to town," said the crewman,

"He is useful. He knows the harbour and the marina. You wait and I will make a few phone calls."

And so, while Bingham made headway among the soups and antipasti, the garlic crostini, the figs and melons, the onion savouries, the sardines and the fish steaks, phone calls were made and the Dutchman's whereabouts discovered. He was a crewman aboard the *Disco Volante* for the duration of the festival.

Bingham had a quiet word with Lina, who said she understood, made his apologies to Patrizio, who assured him his wife would be in good hands, and made his way along the marina towards the *Disco Volante*, the name itself almost a joke along the wharf.

He passed the racing yachts and the large cruisers, where sailors were busy on the decks, swabbing clean the already spotless, lowering or raising flags, coiling sheets, polishing brasses or adding another touch of brilliant white paint to the hulls.

The man who Bingham took to be the owner of the *Disco Volante* was leaning on a brightly varnished wooden rail talking to two women – girls, rather – who were there for the occasion. Their laughter said as much: the hollow laughter of the eager to please.

Bingham couldn't hear what they were saying and the name of the yacht wasn't necessarily a sign of the ownership and so he spoke in English – like it or not, as maybe, the international language.

"Excuse me. Do you have a crewman by the name of Tage Lauwers?"

"Who's asking?"

The rudeness implied in the answer must have amused the girls because they laughed, and the man's smile suggested he was gratified.

"My name is George Bingham. I met Tage yesterday and he was helping me find a missing person."

"Are you a gendarme?"

"No."

"I thought not. You don't sound like a Frenchie."

The man was obviously English and of a rough type: no one with any sensitivity would have used a term intended to be derogatory in a place where French people might overhear. He clearly didn't care – indeed, was enjoying the moment – and the girls laughed again.

"Who are you then?"

"I'm a private investigator. I work for the Société Internationale pour L'application de la Loi. We're allied to Border Control and do some of their footwork," Bingham lied, not quite sure from where the name had sprung.

"You'd better come aboard then. Tage isn't into any trouble is he?"

"On the contrary: he's been most helpful. I just want to check out a few names."

Bingham took the sailor aside when he arrived on deck, out of earshot of the owner or anyone else.

"You're not getting me into trouble are you?"

"No. If you're helpful, your reputation will only be enhanced among the crew by my visit."

"And if I'm not?

Bingham shrugged. He was already tired and in no mood for argy-bargy.

"What do you want?"

"I want you to tell me all you know about La Canape and the people who pass through the bar. I'm looking for the little boy you saw yesterday and I intend to find him. More than anything else, I need names."

"I barely know those people."

"What were you doing there?"

"Enjoying my lunch," replied the Dutchman, giving Bingham his twisted, little smile.

"Don't waste my time. Either decide to help me or tell me to shove off. In which case, we'll make this official."

Bingham repeated the name of the fictitious organisation.

"You said you weren't a detective."

"I'm not. I'm simply an investigator."

"So, the ball ..."

"... was a means of gaining Madame Couchet's confidence. I prefer to work quietly, unofficially, because that way the results come thick and fast. I simply need to learn that the boy is safe – no more. What were you doing at La Canape?"

"I don't know the boy or the woman he was with."

"You've never seen them before?"

"No."

"You must have heard their names."

"Jehane was all I heard. The boy's name wasn't mentioned."

"Did he speak?"

"I told you. They were only there a few minutes. They collected some pastries and went home."

"Where was that?"

"They didn't say."

"What did you make of the boy?"

"Nothing, really. He was quiet."

"Did anyone speak to him?"

"Why would they?"

"Isn't it usual to speak with a child, especially a shy one?"

The Dutchman merely shrugged again.

"Didn't the girl speak to him?"

"I told you …"

"What's her name?"

"How should I know?"

"Because you were well in with that company, sitting comfortably, enjoying a relaxed lunch before the siesta and because you are known for liking woman of *all sorts*."

"Who said that?"

"Don't flannel me. Your reputation is well-known along the marina. How do you think I found you? You're very helpful with *introductions*, they tell me."

"I'm not a pimp."

"I didn't say you were, but you've been around, know a few likely women and bar talk comes easily, doesn't it?"

"All right. Her name is Agnes Lacote."

"Is she a prostitute?"

"Yes."

"Where does she live?"

"There's a small hotel in the Rue Marcelle. I don't know of anywhere else."

"What's her relationship to Madame Couchet?"

"They're friends. Isabelle feels sorry for her. Look, you're getting the wrong end of the stick, friend."

"I'm not grasping either end. I just need names so that I can find the boy. What's the old man's name?"

"Masson – that's all I know."

"Masson Paquet – yes, I've talked with him."

"Then why ask me?"

"I don't want to have to return and I need to know you're telling me the truth. Is there anything else that might help?"

This time, Tage Lauwers thought for a moment before answering, as eager to get rid of Bingham as Bingham was eager to move on.

"No, there's nothing."

"You're sure?"

"Yes."

"Right, now to put your mind at rest, I'll come straight with you. The organisation I mentioned doesn't exist and I am no kind of investigator for anybody. What I said to Madame Couchet, yesterday, was true. What I didn't say was that I'm uneasy about the little boy – and that's all."

"So why the bullshit?"

"It was the only way I could get you to talk. I'm staying at the Majestic and you can contact me there if anything else occurs to you ..."

"I could bloody well throw you overboard."

"But there'd be no point, would there, and if that little boy is where he shouldn't be, you'll be pleased to have helped me."

"What's it got to do with you?"

"What's the wellbeing of children got to do with anyone?"

Bingham felt several pairs of eyes on him as he walked down the gangway. He wasn't sure what Tage Lauwers might do now that he knew Bingham was a nobody, but he needed to tell him: he didn't want Madame Couchet or anyone else to think an official investigation was afoot.

Chapter Five
THE PROSTITUTE

The next morning Bingham woke early, leaving Lina sleeping soundly, and opened his notebook. With any luck, Brockie would have emailed him.

Good Evening, George,

Bearing in mind what you said about how short a time the boy seems to have been in France, I've picked out those cases that have occurred within the past year. Here they are:

Marian Gillet, an English actress who has played bit parts in various soaps, meets her 'dashing French lover' at a Bafta awards party in 2012, they marry in 2013 and almost at once a son is born to them. They are over the moon and we find their photographs in every tabloid.

Two years later, it seems the 'fairy tale romance' is over. There is talk of rows, of the marriage being 'hell on earth', there's an allegation of an attempted kidnap and there is a 'bitter custody battle' and Ms Gillet, now Madame Bizier, turns up at a French police station with injuries to her face. Monsieur Bizier spends the next 48 hours in custody but is then released uncharged.

A lengthy legal battle – still ongoing – ensues as accusation and counter accusations fly back and forth. 'A love story turned to hell' is how one gossip paper calls it. The first court battle ends when both parties are convicted of assault. The judge said that it was impossible to decide who had started the fight but that they had both acted violently.

The second battle is in the family courts, which have awarded custody to both parents, the boy to spend alternate weeks with each. Neither parent must take the boy out of France without the written consent of the other.

An attempt was made by Ms Gillet, who has reverted to her maiden name, to take the boy out of France, but this was intercepted by the border police at a private airfield near Bordeaux. Monsieur Bizier pressed charges for attempted kidnap. Ms Gillet's lawyers claim that she was unaware of the travel restriction, which makes it impossible for her to work and to see her son since her television roles are filmed out of the country.

In another court appearance, Ms Gillet accused Monsieur Bizier of refusing to pay maintenance for his son, an accusation that he vehemently denies.

An elderly lady politely hands over a box of eggs to security guards outside Keswick's Civil Justice Centre. On leaving the building she collects them and waits patiently on the pavement.

When a M Champoux leaves the courtroom, she immediately pelts him with the eggs.

He scrambles to safety by running across the road between oncoming traffic. M Champoux had arrived in court to fight for the right to see his child. He declined to press charges at first but later, on the advice of his lawyer, changed his mind.

The elderly lady, a Mrs Janice Eaves, was arrested and pleaded guilty to the assault. In court, her defence lawyer claimed that she was "extremely unhappy" about judgements about her grandson and that M Champoux, who had been married to her daughter, was planning to kidnap him and take him to France. In mitigation, her lawyer said that "a certain bitterness – a curdling" had crept into the relationship between Mrs Eaves and her son-in-law but went on to say that he had to accept that "on this occasion the defendant had retrieved the eggs from the security guard and thrown them, liberally, at her son-in-law". She now accepted that this was "no way to treat her son-in-law".

Mrs Eaves was bailed prior to sentencing and ordered not to approach M Champoux again.

The next case involves two children, a girl and a boy, but it may be that the lad you are concerned about has a sister somewhere in Britain, and so I have included it.

A five-year-old boy who has been reported missing is believed to be with his father, who is wanted by police for failing to appear in court. Martin Walton was reported missing from Higham, in Kent, on Friday.

Police have said they believe he is with his father, 33-year-old Rene Faucher. He had been due for sentencing on Friday but did not attend the hearing. Officers have not given details of his offence but said a warrant had been issued for his arrest.

Martin is described as having collar-length blonde hair and blue eyes, while Faucher is 5ft 9in and slim, with short brown hair and brown eyes. His sister, Sofia, remains at home in Higham with her mother, Madame Emily Fauchet formerly Walton, who is distraught at her two children being "torn apart in this way".

Chief Inspector Susan Mackenzie said police were "concerned for Martin's whereabouts" and appealed for anyone with information to contact police. "Equally I am issuing a direct appeal for Rene Fauchet to make contact with us to let us know that both he and Martin are safe and well," she said.

You will gather from the tone that this report is taken more or less verbatim from the police handout, George. It is the most recent case and your most likely one, I would think. It is only a month old.

Good Hunting, my friend
Simon

Bingham noticed the Brockie's tone in the two reports he'd written up himself was distinctly different from that of the police handout, and he wondered how a working police officer actually viewed these domestic cases.

He didn't have much patience with the attitudes of the parents concerned. After all, isn't it the parents' business to put the child first, ahead of their own changing feelings for each other? Why commit yourself to bringing a child into the world unless you're sure you have a secure future to offer them, at least while they are children?

Bingham formed no opinion about the three cases. The one advantage they'd given him was names: Bizier, Champoux and Fauchet. Sometime in the next day or so he would hope to come across one of them, but nothing Tage Lauwers had told him tied in with these ones.

He looked across at Lina; she was sound asleep. He looked at his watch; it was barely six o'clock. Cannes would be asleep; at least, the tourists and the holidaymakers would be asleep and those who favoured the night to the day.

Bingham wondered about Agnes Lacote. She owed him nothing. She might have him thrown off the premises; she might even call the police. When all was said and done, he was merely following a feeling, a feeling of unease about a boy he'd seen but once, playing with a toy car, while his grandmother was watching. *Only she wasn't watching.*

The Rue Marcelle wasn't far. He'd leave Lina a note and wander over to the hotel. He knew the kind of place he would find; it was what the French termed a hotel for *un petit moment*. Bingham smiled to himself, but didn't know why; it was, perhaps, a defensive smile, a smile defending his natural feelings of prudery. The French simply didn't view sex in the same light as the English: a right, not a privilege. They arrested their prostitutes, of course, if they had to do so, but the blind eye was preferred. And the eye wasn't always blind, but often wide open in acknowledgement.

The concierge peered at him through the small window of her box room. He didn't look the sort; she could sum a man up in a moment. It only took a glance.

"What do you want?"

"I'm looking for Mademoiselle Lacote. I'm told she sometimes stays here."

"I'll ask."

She spoke into what must once have been a fashionable intercom. It crackled and hissed. Bingham heard a breathless voice though the noise.

"She's not in."

"I need to speak with her. It's urgent."

The woman pressed down the plastic switch a second time and, again, Bingham heard the breathless voice through the static.

"Go up. Room 17."

The door was ajar when Bingham arrived on the landing. He eased it open. Agnes Lacote was standing by the window in a grubby negligee, watching two sparrows chasing each other across the rooftops. On a small bedside table, two wine glasses stood empty. There wasn't much furniture in the room: a small wardrobe, two chairs, on the far side a coffee machine. A silk dressing gown hung on a hook attached to the door.

Agnes Lacote turned and looked at Bingham She was pretty enough or had been until the bloom faded. In the high cheekbones and the full mouth there was promise of what once might have been. Her eyes were still bright, but with the artificial brightness of the drug addict, and her young teeth were already showing signs of loss.

"You're the man who Isabelle threw out of the bar. Get out!"

"I'd appreciate a few words, a few moments of your time."

"Are you the police?"

"No, I'm a tourist, and nothing more."

"I'll call the police."

"By all means. Do you mind if I sit down?"

He wasn't tired – the mornings were the best time of the day for Bingham – but he wanted to put the girl at her ease. They had a name for it in the drama sessions he'd attended. Status: that was the term, and by sitting he was lowering his status. The young woman had become dominant.

"I just wish to have a chat with the little boy and his grandmother. He seemed unhappy."

"Did you speak to him?"

"Yes. Did you?"

"He doesn't speak French."

"That's why I want to speak with him. He seemed lost."

"What's that to you?"

"You're the second person to ask me that question in the space of a few hours. What's the wellbeing of children got to do with anyone?"

"Are you a relative?"

"No, but I have children of my own. I wouldn't want them to be alone in a strange land unable to speak with the people around them. The little boy was frightened."

Agnes turned away, apparently watching the two sparrows. She hadn't bothered to pull together her negligee or cover herself with the dressing gown.

"Who else said that to you?"

"The Dutchman, Tag Lauwers. He's one of your ... friends, isn't he?"

Bingham had only hesitated over the word for a moment, but it was enough.

"He doesn't know anything. Isabelle took pity on him. These foreigners get lonely away from home."

"Do you have any children?"

"What do you think?"

She was easier now: not trusting, but more relaxed. He could hear it in her tone. Bingham doubted whether she ever trusted any man or would ever again. But she was a woman, and Bingham had this old-fashioned idea about women and children.

"Some women do in your position. It's why they take up your kind of work. Do you have a boyfriend?"

"I suppose you might call him that," she replied, with a laugh that just avoided being harsh. "What do you want from me?"

"I have some names. I hoped you might recognise one of them."

"Go on."

"Bizier? ... Champoux? ... Fauchet?"

"No."

"You hesitated. Did one of them ring a bell?"

"No."

"I think it might have done. Does the name Jehane mean anything to you?"

"It's the old woman, Isabelle's friend."

"The one who called at the bar with the boy?"

"Yes."

"Was she his grandmother?"

"Of course, she was."

There was no 'of course' about it, as far as Bingham was concerned, but the girl may have been sincere. How much interest did she take in the comings and goings of Madame Couchet's friends?

"Is the old man, Masson Paquet, often there?"

"You know his name?" asked Agnes, frowning.

"I've spoken with him. He was most helpful."

"You've spoken to him?"

"Yes, I followed him home from La Canape."

"Isabelle won't like that."

"Why? Madame Couchet doesn't have anything to hide, I'm sure."

Agnes was clearly troubled, now, but at the same time relieved, thought Bingham. She was on the verge of a decision. She moved away from the window, took her dressing gown from the door and wrapped it round her.

"Was it Masson who told you where to find Tag?"

"No, that was a crewman aboard *La Fanciulla del West,* a yacht that belongs to a friend of my wife."

"You do get around."

"I try."

"Are you really here on holiday?"

"Yes, my wife's friend is a consultant on a film about Puccini."

"Where is your wife?"

"I left her sleeping. It's very early but I thought I might catch you more easily at this hour."

"You do speak posh. Your French is very good – much better than most English."

"I travelled when I was a young man. I spent some time in your country. I love it."

"How old are your children?"

"Paul is 32, the girls are 31 and Ben is 28."

"Your girls are twins?"

"Yes – Cecilia and Fiorenza. My wife's part-Italian and they're the names of her favourite opera singers."

Agnes had learned more about him, thought Bingham, than he had about her; but she was softening, and he waited.

"I don't know Jehane's name. Isabelle just calls her Jehane, but she has a son. He's got something to do with the film festival. He's called Raimond."

"Thank you. That's most helpful. Do you know if he's married?"

Agnes hesitated. So much always rested in the hesitations, thought Bingham; but what rested this time, he was unsure.

"Not now ... I think ... but he was."

"You knew him?"

"Yes."

It was a flat 'yes', almost dead on her lips.

"He was one of your customers?"

Agnes nodded.

"What's he like – as a person, I mean."

"He's nice. I've said too much! Go away now before you get me into trouble."

"You won't get into trouble through me, Agnes," said Bingham, urgently, almost reaching out and holding her, but deciding against the idea: deciding it might be a gesture misinterpreted. "I promise you."

"You don't know ...Go now. Go now, please."

Bingham stood and moved to the door.

"Please!"

He looked back at the young woman and felt pity. He thought about dropping some money onto her bedside table but thought the move might be resented.

"Thank you, again."

He smiled, closed the door quietly behind him and walked down the stairs. The concierge eyed him as he passed but did not return his smile. On the street, he paused. There was nowhere to sit and he needed to sit somewhere so that he could still the thoughts racing through his head.

He'd known a girl like Agnes once: not a prostitute, just a young woman excited by the freshness of her blossoming sexuality. He'd been young himself, just twenty-one, and wandering around France after he'd left university. He'd known nothing about women at that time; he'd been what they call a 'virgin', although he thought the term foolish when applied to men.

He'd been grape picking in the area near Bordeaux, where the grapes grow on the gravelly soil between the two rivers: the Dordogne and the Garonne. It makes for a crisp, dry, grassy wine but a wine rich and soft: the Entre-Deux-Mers.

She was French and still at university. One evening, after a long day in the fields, they'd taken a walk together and she'd leaned back against a tree and smiled at him. He remembered how her breasts rose and pressed against the singlet she wore; but it was the stare more than anything else that had taken him. She was inviting Bingham to make the move, and he did. Later, he learned that this was the French woman's way: they never made the first move but made it impossible for the man to resist.

It had been a wonderful summer, the summer of '65, and they had loved each other in the way young people do. When the last grape was picked, she had left without saying goodbye. Bingham was heartbroken and had often wondered what became of Michelle.

Chapter Six
THE PIMP

Bingham hadn't walked far before he became aware he was being followed. The step wasn't that of the usual lowlife that mug foreign tourists in any large town or city in the world but that of someone who meant to catch him up and ask questions. It was the step of a man in leather-soled shoes, crisp and sharp on the cobbles, a step that even Bingham heard.

He increased his pace, without appearing to hurry, and made for a street where he'd seen a boulangerie: the morning baguette would call out many locals. As he rounded the corner, he turned, took out the packet of cigarettes he'd bought in case he needed to speak with Masson Paquet again and made as if to light one.

The man walked straight past him, realised what had happened and turned back towards Bingham, who placed the cigarettes back in his pocket and waited.

The man was of the type referred to as rat-faced, although Bingham had always considered the phrase offensive to rats. The look in his eyes suggested he couldn't be trusted out of your sight and the sharpness of his clothes suggested he did little in the way of real work. He was probably intelligent in the way of cunning people: an intelligence of the streets, honed since childhood to assessing every situation in terms of what they could get out of it. Had this been Britain, the man would have had the social security system worked out to a 't', knowing every benefit he was entitled to whether he'd earned it or not, and openly aggressive about his 'entitlement'.

The man's right hand flashed forward and two neatly manicured fingers pointed straight at Bingham's face.

"I've followed you from Hotel Marcelle."

"I rather thought that was the case."

"What were you doing there?"

"What does one usually do in the Hotel Marcelle?"

"You have been with Agnes," said the man, in a tone that was part-question, part-accusation.

"What would that have to do with you?"

Unless the man lived very close to the hotel, possibly in it, Agnes would not have had time to phone him after Bingham left and for the man to be on the street; even then, he would have had to be already dressed.

"I take it the concierge phoned you," he said, "Why? It cannot be strange for Mademoiselle Lacote to entertain customers, can it? And I repeat, what has it to do with you?"

"I am her protector."

"You mean her pimp?"

"We have to look after ourselves in these streets. You know that."

Why the assumption? It suddenly occurred to Bingham that the pimp took him to be a local or, at least, a Frenchman. He found that comforting.

"My name is Henri Faron," said Bingham, "and I'm not used to being questioned, in the street especially, by a complete stranger. Perhaps you'd better introduce yourself and state your business, quickly."

"My name is no concern of yours, Monsieur Faron."

"Then, I'll bid you good day," replied Bingham, stepping out onto the street as though to cross to the boulangerie.

The man's arm shot out and grabbed Bingham by the elbow. It was a hard grip, one that nipped and tightened. The nails dug into his arm through his jacket. The pimp's nose twitched and one side of his mouth jerked up, revealing a set of teeth whose condition in no way matched the care shown by his clothes.

Bingham wasn't bothered by the obvious threat, but it made him think of Agnes Lacote and the life she led with this man. It wasn't the first time his investigations had put others in danger. He looked up and down the street.

"There is a bar over the way. Let's talk in there," he said.

The pimp's grip loosened and he followed Bingham to the bar, where those men who set out for work early were already downing the morning cognac. They looked up as Bingham and the pimp entered and exchanged glances that suggested they knew the latter.

The barman, a tired-looking man wearing a waistcoat over a check shirt held at the throat by a bow tie, pushed the brandies towards them over the polished, wooden counter and Bingham led the pimp to a table in the corner where they overlooked the street.

"Now," he said, "state your interest in me and I'll try to satisfy it."

"I am Agnes Lacote's protector and ..."

"Why did the concierge make a point of calling you?"

"She was suspicious about your purpose. You don't look like the ... usual type of client that Agnes attracts."

"She thought I might harm Mademoiselle Lacote?"

The pimp froze, as though the very question was naïve. Why should he care over-much if the girl was harmed? It was one of the everyday risks she took on his behalf.

"No, she did not think you were *un pervers*.

It was the first time Bingham had heard the French phrase for 'pervert'. He'd never really understood the French attitude towards prostitution. In his youth, an English teacher had told him that it was "simply accepted. The French do not look upon sex as 'dirty' the way we do in Protestant countries. It is a fact of life. The wife says she has a headache and advises you to 'go and see Maisie down the road'." Bingham remembered being shocked and, truth to tell, still felt the same, but quietly.

"She was right. My interest in Mademoiselle Lacote was not sexual. I am looking for a child the British have reason to believe has been kidnapped and brought to France. I bumped into mademoiselle at a local bar two days ago, a customer there told me where she worked and I asked her if she could give me some names. She was loyal to her friends, but helpful."

The mixture of lies, half-truths and actual truths in his explanation amazed Bingham. Lina would have been quite upset hearing them trip so readily from his tongue; her English Catholic upbringing brooked no place for lies unlike, he felt, the French one, which seemed to accept them as one accepts the fact of the frailty of mankind.

"What did she tell you?"

"Nothing that needs to frighten, or even trouble, you."

Bingham had no intention of mentioning Raimond, Jehame's son, because the pimp would consider that to be the betrayal of a customer, possibly a valuable one.

"I do not think I shall need to speak with Mademoiselle Lacote again, but I may look her up to assure myself that she is well. I would not wish to think of her coming to harm because of my visit. Do you understand me?"

"I shall do what is necessary."

The remark was thrown off with a swagger of the pimp's shoulders, a swagger that suggested he did what he liked and no one dared to question him.

"I work for Les Renseignements Generaux – you understand?" said Bingham.

The pimp paled. He knew of the RG, a political police force, an arm of the Interior Minister that gathered information, secretly, on people likely to be a nuisance to the government; the RG were people who filed reports on their neighbours, and not the kind of body to appeal to the pimp and his sort.

"Now, is there anything else you wish to know? Good. Then go."

The pimp left the bar. Bingham hoped he'd scared him sufficiently to save Agnes any trouble. The pimp seemed the kind of man who might enjoy giving a woman a good beating.

*

When he got back to the Majestic, Lina and Patrizio were enjoying their breakfast. Bingham caught Lina's eye before Patrizio had noticed him and laughed. The humour was not lost on his wife.

"I'm sorry, Patrizio. Did Lina explain? Of course, she did."

"Have you had breakfast, Bing?" asked Lina.

"No ... um, a croissant and black coffee would be wonderful."

"This is the man, Patrizio, who always enjoys a cooked breakfast at home."

"When in Rome ...," replied Bingham, "or, in this case, Cannes."

"You have a good life with the beautiful Lina, do you not."

Patrizio spoke in his native language and his comment wasn't a question: it was taken as read that any man living with Lina Marinacci, as she had been called when Patrizio knew her as a student, would be having a good life.

"It's a wonderful life," replied Bingham, "I have been a very lucky man, and sometimes it frightens me."

"Why?" asked Patrizio.

"I'm superstitious about pushing my luck, and sometimes I feel that the whole fabric of our life together might crumble. No one deserves such luck as mine or such love as I have found ..."

"You Protestants are all the same," laughed Patrizio, "You are fearful of the good life, of enjoying yourselves, as if God will punish you if you delight in the pleasure of living. Hmm?"

It was a question, this time. The Italian was asking Bingham to explain his reservations about the pursuit of pleasure in all its forms.

"I do not like taking life for granted."

"It is your English timidity speaking, George. You should embrace life, take it with strength, and hold it to your heart as you would a beautiful woman."

"You sound remarkably French, if I may say so, Patrizio. Perhaps it's the air of Cannes?" said Lina.

Patrizio smiled indulgently and tapped her gently on the arm.

"You have a point," said Bingham, "and I don't dispute it, but it's also a question of styles of masculinity, the gentle against the tough, and I have never been tough when it comes to women or to life."

Lina looked at him as he spoke and a feeling passed between, spoken only with the eyes.

"You are well in with the festival organisers, I imagine, are you not?" Bingham asked Patrizio, changing the subject in that way he had of doing.

"I know many, of course," replied Patrizio with a shrug.

"You have no plans for this morning, Lina tells me. I wonder, then, if you can help me. I'm trying to find a man, possibly the father of the boy I told you about. I only know his first name, which is Raimond – not much to go on, I know, but a man with your connections …," said Bingham, who also shrugged, "and he would be a local with a family in the area, likely to have been married – possibly still married – to a British woman, he would have spent some time in the UK, he may have a reputation for being a womaniser…"

*

"You are a devil, Bing," said Lina, later, as they walked together along the marina, gazing at the unreal boats crowded together along the wharf and stretching far out into the Mediterranean, where they became little more than dots against the blues of sky and water.

"Not at all. Patrizio will enjoy the hunt."

"It's quite a task you've set him, and it was deliberate."

"I'm quite desperate to find this man, Lina, and I'm prepared to try any means. There's just a chance that your friend will come up with something. If nothing else, he is persistent."

"And if he doesn't?"

"I asked the concierge at the hotel when you went up to get ready. He is a man like Patrizio and his masculinity depends upon his success. Besides he is a concierge, and they are always a force to be reckoned with. Do you remember the one in Boston at the Hilton on Broad Street – John McKinnon, was his name, if I remember correctly?"

Lina did. They'd arrived at the airport to find only one, small car available: not the one they'd ordered. The hire company's employees hadn't given a stuff and two mornings later, when they were about to start their drive through New England, Bingham had found the petrol tank almost empty and the car in need of oil. The attitude of the hire staff had been along the lines that if the Binghams cared to bring the car back to the airport they might take a look and they might see if they could find the car Bingham had ordered. This Bingham refused to do, having braved the Boston rush hour two days before. It was at that point the hotel concierge took over the conversation, and within the hour the Binghams had the car they'd ordered, fully tanked with petrol and oil, and they were on their way.

"You sent him a bottle of whisky, didn't you?"

"Yes, I'll get Patrizio a case of Barolo."

"He is nice, Bing."

"I know, and I'm not jealous, so don't think it ... but my money's on the concierge."

"It was a nice little speech you made at breakfast. It's one reason I love you."

Bingham kissed his wife and remembered all those years ago. At the back of his mind was the thought that it couldn't be true and that one day soon he'd wake up to find her gone.

"There has always come a moment in the very few cases I've been involved with when a truth comes home to rest. It's not always apparent what it is at the time but this morning, listening to Patrizio, a thought occurred to me that seems to explain the plight of that little boy."

Lina looked at Bingham and waited. They'd turned from the Croisette and were walking along the wharf towards a little café where coffee was brewed as only the French can brew it.

"It was about men. There are many kinds, of course, and we will not be stereotyped, but ... he touched on two distinct types ...or styles if you prefer the term. How would you describe the French type, Lina?"

"Libidinous? They're the type that French women – and Italian women, for that matter – seem to admire ... well, perhaps *expect* is a more exact way of saying it."

"And that was the thought, maybe the truth, which occurred to me."

Chapter Seven

THE FATHER

Bingham was right: by lunchtime, the concierge had found his man. Raimond Chaput was the founder and owner of one of the firms involved with publicity and printing in connection with the festival. The concierge was able to supply the address of the firm, but Bingham would understand if he offered no personal information about Monsieur Chaput, wouldn't he? Bingham would and was grateful.

Wishing Lina and Patrizio another interesting session watching the Cannes hopefuls, Bingham set out for the address the concierge had provided. The print works had an impressive frontage: modern yet tasteful, blending perfectly with the surrounding residences and yet proclaiming boldly that 'Chaput and Son, Printers' was a progressive firm offering up-to-the-minute publicity materials.

The windows drew in light from the Rue Boningue and lit the neat, little, glass-topped desk at which a secretary was busy word-processing. She looked up as Bingham entered and smiled. To Bingham's mind, she was very French, the French of the Mediterranean coast: olive-skinned with a sheaf of dark brown hair that managed to drape itself round her bare shoulders as if a god somewhere had intended it to rest there forever.

"Monsieur?"

Bingham loved the way in which the intonation of a word conveyed it as a statement or a question. The Italians had it as well as the French but it was, somehow, missing with his own language.

"Would it be possible to have a few words with Monsieur Chaput, please?"

The young woman did not ask if he had an appointment but picked up the phone and spoke quite casually to whoever answered her call. She raised her eyebrows and smiled at Bingham. It was enough.

"Bingham," he said, "George Bingham."

She repeated the name into the mouthpiece, listened with that smile on her lips and then turned to Bingham.

"Monsieur Chaput is occupied for a little while but if you could wait?"

Bingham smiled his thanks and the young woman, whose name he had seen on her desk as Odette Duffet, led him to a comfortable seat in the corner by the window where he could enjoy the view and the cup of black coffee she placed on the occasional table in front of him.

It was less than fifteen minutes before Raimond Chaput appeared through a door behind and slightly to one side of Mademoiselle Duffet. They smiled at each other, the easy smile of people who worked together and liked each other.

"Thank you, Odette ... I'm sorry to have kept you waiting, Monsieur Bingham. How may I help you?"

It was only at that moment, met with such felicitousness, that Bingham realized he had no business to be where he was at all. Who was he to pry into the private life of this young man?

Raimond Chaput appeared to be in his late thirties. His face bore an amiable smile, not one assumed for the moment but quite genuine and expressing the intention to be helpful.

"It's a private matter, Monsieur Chaput. If we could …"

"Of course," replied the owner of the printing firm, leading Bingham out through the small door and along a short corridor before climbing a narrow flight of stairs to a little office that was crammed with machinery and stacks of paper and boxes of ink cartridges. The contrast with the calm of the frontage made Bingham smile, a smile not missed by Raimond Chaput, who returned it without explanation.

He was of slim build and obviously fit. The suit he wore was smart enough to welcome customers and practical enough to administer the workplace. Bingham only had to watch the man in his own element to know that he was in charge of a well-run establishment where employees were content and where they were likely to see out their working lives. He was finding it increasingly difficult to come to the point and his hesitation clearly puzzled the young man.

Bingham took the seat offered and looked up at Raimond Chaput, who perched on a desk that had been thrust back into a corner to make way for a computerised printer that was in stark contrast to an ancient, hand-operated ink roller machine that stood against the far wall.

Feeling forced to speak in a situation where he would have been more comfortable simply observing, Bingham outlined the reason for his visit.

"Has my wife sent you? Are you a private detective?"

The questions, though blunt, were not uttered impolitely: the young man merely sought clarification.

"No, I am here on no one's behalf but my own."

"And my son's."

"Ye-es."

"I believe you, Mr Bingham, but you will, I think, agree that you are a most unusual fellow."

Bingham wasn't sure whether Raimond Chaput had chosen the word deliberately or not. There was nothing in French that matched 'fellow' and the Frenchman had chosen Bingham's own language, which he spoke with the usual accent that English women found so attractive. Whatever the reason, there was no mockery in the use of the word: more an attempt at chumminess.

Under such circumstances, Bingham felt unable to go into his attendant concerns, namely the company the 'grandmother' kept: the owner of a questionable bar, a prostitute, her pimp, one of her customers, a senile old man with what sounded like a mad wife in an upstairs room.

"I mean no offence to your mother, Monsieur Chaput."

"I take none. You see a four-year old child clearly uncomfortable and unhappy in his surroundings and with the company he finds himself in, and you worry and you search for an answer. I take it that you have not spoken with my mother other than the few words you exchanged on the Croisette?"

"No. I was not sure until now that the lady was the boy's grandmother."

"Perhaps you should speak with her and put your mind at rest?"

Bingham wasn't sure whether the remark was a question or a suggestion. At home, it would have been tinged with sarcasm, but this was absent from the Frenchman's tone. Listening to the young man and watching him, Bingham wondered whether he was simply being evasive.

"I can give you her address if you wish, but approach gently, Mr Bingham. My mother, too, is uncomfortable with the situation in which she finds herself and I do not want her alarmed. I will be pleased to see her first to forewarn her – if that is not too harsh a term."

"I have no right …"

"No, no! I would wish to put your mind at rest. Someone as resourceful as you will not let this matter rest until he is certain of his assurances … Mr Bingham, it is late for lunch. Have you eaten?"

"No."

"Nor I … We are working full out at the moment and I missed mine. Let me take you to my local brasserie. We will find sandwiches there and a beer. There we can talk quietly."

Passing through the reception area, Raimond Chaput spoke briefly to Odette Duffet, who smiled a response, and led Bingham along a few side streets to the Brasserie Bleu, where he nodded briefly at the patron who arrived at the table, after a short while, with a tray of sandwiches and two beers.

"Merci, Daniel."

"You have spent some time in Britain," said Bingham, who by now had collected himself together and stayed with his own language.

"In England, mainly, yes. We have secured a significant amount of work in your country – now threatened, we feel, with this Brexit nonsense."

"I'm as sad – angry – as you," replied Bingham, "Europe needs to be strong, politically, and is stronger with Britain as a member."

"You are right, although my interests are largely commercial ... I like you, Mr Bingham, and I trust you for some reason I have yet to explain to myself ... but that is why we are here. It is important to me that you leave Cannes with a good impression of me and mine. Please, eat while we talk."

Bingham found a cheese sandwich with lettuce and tomato, and tucked in. French sandwiches were small and the flavours came through. There had been a time when the word 'vegetarian' in France had meant 'one who ate pork' and he was surprised to have found a sandwich he could enjoy so readily.

"I met Amanda Eaves when I was seeking a liaison with a printer in a small town in your Lake District, Keswick by name. It was the purest coincidence. I had been taken to a local theatre by the owner of the printing firm we were hoping to work with, and there she was. Quite a charming woman – or so I thought at the time – but one who had yet to meet what she called 'Mr Right'.

"I spent more time there than I might have done. We began to communicate. She came over to France and I met her in Paris. The English believe Paris is France, I think. Eventually, she even came to Cannes – not to the festival, I might say, which she considered 'a playground for the rich and idle and vulgar', but to spend time with me.

"She was a woman waiting to be conquered – if you understand my meaning."

Bingham thought he did. It had seemed to him as a youth, and he'd not changed his mind since, that to the French – French men, in particular – that love – or, more precisely, sex – was a game played in the pursuit of pleasure.

"I pursued her vigorously, and it was clear that she was flattered, she enjoyed the chase and, I must confess, I was skilful. It was not long before she surrendered herself and we became lovers. She was what you call a feminist, but the word is meaningless in my country: a woman is a woman, you know, a beautiful creature to be pursued and conquered. Even so – and, perhaps, this was part of the attraction – she wanted to be dominated.

"For us French, love is an art form – you understand?"

Eager not to break the flow of this man's disclosures, Bingham nodded. Was 'disclosure' the word? It certainly wasn't a confession, but more a statement of fact. To an English ear, what Raimond had to say bordered on the boastful, but Bingham hesitated to make that judgment.

"Sex is a form of pleasure for us that can never be replicated by descending into the culture of drugs and alcohol so common in your country. So, it was for Amanda and for me. It was my desire to ... sublimate my joy in marriage to her and so Mathieu was born to us."

So that was the little boy's name: Mathieu Chaput. And yet he was so English: Bingham had no doubt that was so. Since he was four, Mathieu would have been born in 2014, and conceived in 2013? Such a short time ago, and so much had happened.

"My father's name," said Raimond, "You saw the sign above our works – 'Chaput and Son'. I am the son. Amanda wanted 'Matthew' but I insisted.

"Were you married in France?"

"Naturally. I proposed to Amanda in a Parisian restaurant. She could not resist. Ten months after we were married, Mathieu was with us."

Bingham wondered, perhaps ungenerously, what had held him up. He polished off his first beer and two more appeared with another collection of sandwiches, variations on the pan-bagnat topped with combinations of green salad, tomatoes, hard-boiled eggs, tuna, anchovies, cucumbers, fava beans, artichokes, green peppers, radishes, onions, basil, and black olives.

He waited for the downward spiral of the conversation. There had to be one: after all, the marriage was barely five years old and the couple were, presumably, living apart. Or had he jumped to the wrong conclusion? Was Raimond setting him up for a just humiliation?

"Why am I telling you this, Mr Bingham?"

"I have no idea. Perhaps you wish to justify – no, explain – a different cultural ... perspective?"

"Perhaps I do ... I did not ... abandon – is that the word? – my ... perspective, as you phrase it ... I felt that the ... marriage had reached its peak."

Raimond looked at Bingham, and the latter remained breathless.

"You were caught in a trap," he said, eventually, eager for the Frenchman to continue.

"Possibly."

"But one of your own making?"

Raimond Chaput looked at Bingham as though he were the saviour of the moment.

"You have an understanding of our culture, Mr Bingham?"

"I try."

"I had no contempt for Amanda – you understand this?"

"Yes."

"But ... the moment had passed. We were no longer ... I am not a compulsive philanderer – you understand – but ... I may have been ... imprudent ..."

The very word amused Bingham: imprudent – what could Raimond Chaput mean to convey by his use of the word?

"It was the mother who caused the trouble: but for her Amanda would have been content."

Bingham guessed what the Frenchman meant but wanted clarification and didn't like to ask for it: such a question, he felt, would set their rapport back.

"The mother ...," he asked, leaving the pause hanging.

"She saw me, one day, with Diana ... But for her ... It was all over then. If only we had been in France."

"Surely, the truth would have ... emerged, eventually?"

"Would she have wanted to know?" asked Raimond.

"Amanda?"

"Of course."

"I think she might have wanted to know the truth."

"The truth is ... relative. You English think too much of it."

The thought of being unfaithful to his wife had never occurred to Bingham – indeed, the very idea would have repulsed him – but of one thing he was sure, although it was not something he'd ever thought about, and that was that Lina would very certainly have wanted to know the truth.

Raimond Chaput smiled at Bingham, and the smile broke into a laugh.

"Excuse me, Mr Bingham, I am not laughing at you, but the expression on your face tells me all. What is it your Lady Macbeth said – 'it is a face where men may read strange things'?"

"Something of the sort," replied Bingham, thinking more of the 'serpent under it'."

"My father was a wonderful man, Mr Bingham. Everyone adored him, including my mother. He was a successful businessman and a notable person in the town. You can see for yourself what he has left behind him. He was not a compulsive philanderer, you understand, but he adored women. There were those in the town who knew him well and he was ... attentive to them.

"He was an impulsive man. Once, I remember, he caught one of our housemaids bending. She complained to my mother, who laughed it off. "What do you expect from Mathieu?" she said. She knew, you see, but it is the way with us not to let these matters divide the family. There was no way my father was to be brought low by these women. Such matters are of less importance than in your country."

"But Amanda took a somewhat different view?"

"She threw me out. You can imagine how devastated I was without my Mathieu. She refused to let me see him, to even say goodnight to my little boy. My world crumbled about me. I came home ..."

"You were living in England at the time?"

"We had houses in both places. It was there that the mother-in-law saw me. I had to leave Diana, too, of course."

"Of course," replied Bingham, hoping his tone did not reveal that his mind was living, temporarily at least, in another universe.

"I could not allow such a thing to go on. I could not live apart from my family."

"You tried for reconciliation?"

"There was no chance of that happening – Amanda is not a woman of the world – but I had to get my son back. You understand?"

The constant question of whether Bingham understood was not a search for assurance – Raimond's English was clear – his command of the language was admirable – but more that Bingham was sympathetic to his behaviour and his subsequent plight.

"I was without my son for so long. I tried the right way – through the courts – but Amanda would not allow him out of the country, and my work was here. When it came – the time to fetch my boy – it was easy, unbelievably easy. I was so relieved. Diana was a great help, naturally."

"Naturally," said Bingham.

"I was known at the day nursery where Amanda had Mathieu looked after almost from the day he was born. I visited several times. The staff understood. On the day we chose, Diana came with me. It is always good to have a woman at such times. We collected him at lunchtime and drove away. They knew me on the cross ferry. I was a familiar figure, coming and going and this time I had my little boy. I mean to keep him, Mr Bingham."

"Your wife will try to get him back. Has she done so yet?"

"We are waiting and we are … keeping him close. My mother is a great help. I trust you, Mr Bingham. I need you to understand."

Bingham, quite unwillingly, felt he had Raimond Chaput cornered. He had offered an explanation because it was the only course open to him. Bingham wondered how soon it would be before the authorities discovered the child's whereabouts. Surely they must know he was with his father and that the father lived and worked in Cannes.

"What were your access rights?" he asked.

"As I said, Mathieu was not to leave the UK."

"Has your wife been in touch?"

"We take no calls from her, either at home or at work. Odette has heard her down the phone but Odette is a wise girl and manages the anger with great calm."

"But your wife must know where Mathieu is."

"Yes, but … how shall I say it? I am known here in Cannes. The Police Judiciaire will not impose upon me unnecessarily."

Bingham smiled at the word. The British always supposed it was they who had invented bureaucracy, but the French were not far behind, if not actually ahead.

"Our greatest concern is not someone like you, but someone who is paid to find Mathieu and snatch him from us – a private agent."

"As you snatched him from your wife," replied Bingham, not meaning the words to sound as abrupt as they did but knowing that somewhere in Britain a mother was grieving for her lost child, an attractive boy with large, green eyes and a wonderfully shaped head. "My concern has placed me in a difficult position, Monsieur Chaput."

"There is always the blind eye, Mr Bingham, the salve of so many wives whose husbands have interests elsewhere."

"Such as your mother?"

"Such as my mother, as you say. The old lady you saw with Mathieu is not the woman she was when she soothed the housemaid. My father's death aged her, and I do not want to hasten further that process."

"No, of course not. You say I may speak with your mother?"

"Of course. Here," replied Raimond, writing the address on the back of an envelope he took from his inner pocket, "You see how we trust you."

The two men, so different in kind, shook hands at the door of the brasserie, and went on their respective ways: Chaput to his work, Bingham to wander the side of the marina until it was time to meet Lina.

He knew how she would have felt if one of her children had been snatched, even by Bingham, following the breakup of their marriage, a circumstance – thank God, thought Bingham – that never happened or seemed like happening.

As it was, he now knew where Amanda Chaput lived without having to investigate the matter further. Chaput – Champoux. To the ear of an English journalist, especially a journalist eager to get their story to press, the names would have sounded much the same and the spelling must have been guesswork.

Bingham hadn't mentioned the story because he didn't want to alarm Chaput or give him reason to think that Bingham knew more about the case than was apparent and was really the agent he feared; but he felt sure that Raimond Chaput, the grand seducer, must be the man who a mother-in-law had pelted with eggs.

Chapter Eight
THE MISTRESS

In a way, Bingham made up his mind even as the two of them shook hands, but he wanted to consult Lina, although he knew what she would say.

Truth to tell, he felt a little lost, awash in a strange world, a world where the mores of the people were so different from his own and his own kind. He'd liked Raimond Chaput, while at the same time being repelled by him; except for the pimp, who he disliked unconditionally, he'd liked, with slight reservations, all the people he'd met – the prostitute, the sailor, the patronne, the grandmother and the old man.

He made his way to the marina, where all thoroughfares seemed to lead, and gazed at the yachts. He'd looked up Cannes before they came and knew that it was the beginning of the French Riviera, a stretch of coastline almost forty miles long: villas, yachts, casinos and hotels all preceded by the word 'luxury'.

Yet this term had not applied to the people he'd met and spoken with apart from Chaput, perhaps. There he was, making exceptions again! He was comfortable with the notion, the idea, that people, while sharing a similar outlook on life, were all different, all unique in their own way and that this applied to races as well as individuals – and yet!

'Yet' – that word again! Bingham felt like a teenage boy struggling to come to terms with the beliefs of his parents while holding others, sometimes inimical to theirs, of his own. His experiences in Cannes were reviving memories of the time he'd spent in France over fifty years ago. But this time, they weren't experiences that just affected him: how he reacted to them impinged on the livelihood, the welfare, of a little boy.

"Mr Bingham".

Again, the tone that could have meant comment or question. He looked up. The woman who had spoken was one whose beauty would have frozen him to the spot as a young man: it was unapproachable. She had icy blue eyes, immaculately coiffured hair and a smile, a feminine smile, which saw right through him. Bingham was sure he blushed.

"I didn't mean to startle you."

"I've no idea how long I've been standing here," he said, "I was miles away."

"My father's the same," replied the woman, "May I have a word with you? My name is Nicole Lenard. I am Raimond Chaput's mistress."

Could Bingham believe his ears? He thought not.

"I'm sorry to come upon you like this but I'm concerned for Raimond."

"He didn't send you after me."

Bingham realised his own tone now covered question and comment. It wasn't a question: he knew a man like Chaput would do no such thing.

"No, no, of course not. When he returned to the office, Odette saw how troubled he was and gave me a ring."

"How did you find me?"

"I was lucky. Most tourists make for the marina and Odette's description was very accurate. You're a man of distinguished appearance, Mr Bingham."

"It's the grey hair," he replied, with an embarrassed laugh.

"You're not overly tall, but you are erect for a man of your age."

"Your English is very good, Madame Lenard. I don't think I've heard that lovely word 'overly' used in conversation at home for years."

"Our education system is second to none, Mr Bingham. It is rigorous. I was educated at what you would call a state school, L'Ecole Publique, and I think my English is superior to the French of your Eton-educated politicians."

"I'm sure you're right," replied Bingham with a slight bow.

"May we speak of Raimond?"

Bingham didn't feel like another bar or café and so he led the way to one of the seats overlooking the marina. The sun was warm as was the slight breeze from the Mediterranean, and it was pleasant sitting there together, immersed in what a passer-by would interpret as intimate conversation. They could have been a couple: a sugar-daddy with his young mistress.

Not that Nicole Lenard was all that young: he guessed her to be near Raimond in age, but she was one of those women who retain the facial vigour of their youth. She possessed high cheekbones and a full mouth that seemed to purse when Nicole was about to speak. Her icy eyes never left Bingham's as she spoke.

"I feel you may have the wrong idea about Raimond. He is not a licentious man. He is a Frenchman, a man brought up in a world far away from your own and the expectations of him are not those of men like you. In France, women are to be adored and pursued. We are not caught up with the feminist claptrap, the battle of the sexes, which bedevils men and attractive women in your country.

"We wish to be admired as women. We celebrate, we do not hide, the difference. If a man treats us as anything but desirable, we are offended, and he is less than a man. We are brought up to be desired and men, to desire.

"Raimond and I have known each other on and off for many years. When he returned to Cannes I could see how unhappy he was. I cherish him. His marriage to the Englishwoman was a mistake. He is not a man who can bear coldness. He needs to be loved."

Bingham wanted to ask questions but didn't like to interrupt this woman, not so much because her flow was so telling, but more that he didn't want to set her back on her heels: questioning might suggest disbelief.

"I was always attracted to Raimond and when he returned that desire was, again, overwhelming. I lost no time displaying my feelings, encouraging him to make the first move."

Was Nicole aware that he had a mistress in England? Had he told her about Diana or did he think she wouldn't want to know? How permanent did she envisage her affair (was that the word?) with Raimond to be? Marriage? Children? Did these considerations enter her mind?

"Raimond and I could have a good life here in Cannes," said Nicole, as though reading Bingham's thoughts, "He is a wealthy man and well-connected."

She looked at Bingham wondering, he thought, whether all she was saying had sunk in. She was here to persuade him not to rock the boat. As though he could! Chaput's problems lay with the courts.

"And we can give Mathieu a good life – and a good education. He will be surrounded with love, Mr Bingham."

"You think I might seek out the mother when I return to England and, knowing what I know, lead her directly to Mathieu and another kidnap or, worse still from your point of view, hours spent in courtrooms arranging access?"

"I fear for Raimond."

"Have you ever been married, Madame Lenard?"

"Once, but my husband was placed in an impossible position," she replied, looking at Bingham as though he should understand what she meant.

"Go on."

"He discovered my affair. He could not tolerate it."

"I see. Do you plan on being faithful to Raimond?"

"Naturally."

"Do you have children of your own?"

"One little girl – she is adorable."

"And benefitting from a rigorous education at one of your L'Ecole Publique?"

Nicole Lenard smiled.

"Were you a teacher, Mr Bingham?"

"Yes."

"I thought so. I do so love your English sarcasm. It is a shield – yes? Do your children – I can tell you have children – have a thorough knowledge of your country's history and literature? Are they fluent in at least two languages, including their own? Are they familiar with the writings of the philosophers of the Western world?"

Bingham wasn't sure. His four children had read extensively. He supposed his two girls, Cecilia and Fiorenza, one a politician's secretary and the other a researcher for the BBC, were literate; he supposed his older son, Paul, a doctor, knew something about medicine and the human body; he supposed his younger son, Ben, a chemist, knew a thing or two about the properties of substances.

"They all speak Italian, fluently," he replied, "and could make their way round Germany, Spain and your own country, but their grasp on our own history might be patchy and as for philosophers, I'm not sure."

Bingham, as a former teacher, wasn't one who valued knowledge merely for its own sake.

"You do not have philosophers of any standing, do you, except, perhaps, Bertrand Russell. Your language is extensive but not precise. Your wife is Italian?"

"Yes – well, her mother was and we all speak it."

"You surprise me, Mr Bingham. I had you down as a traditional type of Englishman."

"I think my wife might agree with you."

"There you go again, saying what you do not mean."

"You never asked me how good my children were at mathematics," said Bingham, smiling, eager to take command of the conversation.

"You know my country better than I realised."

"I travelled widely as a youth – across Europe as a whole."

"You met your wife in Italy?"

It was a question, this time. Nicole Lenard was curious about Bingham's wife. Brought up to be seductive, she naturally saw other women as rivals even when – as must be the case between she and Lina – they were not.

"No," replied Bingham, keen to offer as little information as politeness allowed.

"Then where?"

"At an English opera in an English theatre."

"There are such things as English operas?"

At home, the remark would have been intended as ironic but, in Nicole's case, Bingham knew this wasn't so.

"Lina was an opera singer?"

Again, a question intended as such.

"Yes."

"You saw her sing and you fell in love with her?"

"No, we … met in the foyer. We were both at a loose end."

He didn't know why he'd added that last remark, why he needed to play down the moment their eyes had met, but he did know that Lina felt no need to go on proving herself as he felt Nicole Lenard did. Must French women always remain beautiful and seductive? Were there no years, later in life, when they might relax and welcome the blessings of old age? Lina had friends, and she was not in competition with them, whereas Bingham thought that Nicole would always be looking over her shoulder, wondering whether she or another was the more beautiful and desirable.

He began to like her and his attraction to this woman stirred his pity, a pity he knew she'd reject as an insult.

"I can promise you nothing, Madame Lenard," he said, "except this – I will act in Mathieu's interests and in the interests of no other. Will that ease your mind?"

"No, Mr Bingham. I wish you to act in the interests of Raimond."

"Then we must hope that his interests are those of his son's, and that I understand them both."

Their parting was not amicable. Nicole rose coldly, looked down at him along the bridge of her elegant nose and walked – stalked, thought Bingham – off along the quayside.

He watched her trim figure become smaller and then disappear beyond the tourists and the celebrity boats. He'd added another person to his list of people he liked but who, also, occasioned in him a sense of disapproval.

Bingham wondered about the mother, Amanda Chaput nee Eaves, and Diana, the Keswick mistress, and decided to email his ex-policeman friend, Simon Brockie.

*

Evening was approaching when he met Lina, alone, on the quayside exactly where they'd met the previous afternoon, and she knew at once that he was troubled. As always with her, Lina came directly to the point.

"Bing, what's wrong"

"Can we go for a drink? I know a little café on the Rue Meynadier."

Sitting outside the little café Bingham had found on his first morning, Lina with a traditional Kir, Bingham with a local red, Lina looked about her and then leaned across the table towards her husband.

"Well?"

Bingham told her of his two meetings: the father whose wife had thrown him out, the mistress desperate to reclaim him.

"I've never been taken with the 'two homes' idea, Lina."

"You mean the kind of people who claim the child has two homes and, therefore, twice the benefits when a couple break up?"

"Yes. It's been my experience that a child would prefer to be in the one home with their father and mother together ... I know what you're thinking, Lina – that I should face reality, that couples do break up, there's no help for it and the children should accept the fact. Better two happy homes than one angry one."

"I was thinking nothing of the sort. I agree with you, but I'm not sure I'd have put up with you having a mistress. I'm putting myself in Amanda Eaves's place."

"We never really had any issues to face, did we?"

"I wouldn't say that: you were too soft on the children, and it was always me who took the firm hand. Also, we were both set in our ways when we got together – you were forty and I was thirty-five. Our habits were entrenched. What we did was turn a blind eye to our differences, differences that many couples let fester. Was this Diana really his mistress or was it a one-off mistake?"

"I don't know. Brockie's looking into it for me."

"You liked Raimond Chaput, didn't you?"

"Yes."

"You're wondering whether Amanda should have thrown him out? ... Some men just *must* take up the challenge – if you want to put it that way. I mean, Patrizio made a pass at me, today, but it was his way of paying a compliment, part of his charm."

"I expect he did: you're an attractive woman. Were you enticing him?"

"What do you mean?"

"You're very open, Lina: you hug, and you kiss and welcome people with your eyes and your smile. You have a loving nature and it's clear in your mannerisms: you are a touchy-feely person."

"I'm sixty-nine, Bing."

"You're still an attractive woman. What happened?"

"We were having a drink after the film, a little bar – very sedate, very respectable, and we sat at a corner table. I think he was taken with the moment."

"Past memories?"

"Yes, he reached over, took my hand very gently and kissed it."

"I don't blame him."

That evening, Patrizio was charm itself. The meal, despite Patrizio going for the blanquette de veau while Lina and Bingham stayed with coquilles st-jacques, was a delight; and, later, the three of them strolled along the esplanade arm in arm.

*

Brockie's call came through the following morning.

"She was easy enough to find, George, and 'very tasty' as we used to say in the old days. I got in touch with a journalist on the local rag. Journalists tend to know anyone who might have appeared in the papers and they have a long memory.

"This Diana Hart works in one of the gourmet pubs, as they call them these days, and I could see what the attraction was for your Raimond. Imagine Michelle Pfeiffer behind the bar pulling pints and you get the picture."

"Are you phoning from home, Brockie?"

"Why?"

"I'm wondering whether Aileen is listening in."

"She's away visiting her sister, which is what gave me the chance to visit Keswick. Don't worry, George, I'm not the suicidal type. Shall I go on, now?"

"Yes. Thanks."

"What he had with this Diana was what we used to call 'a fling'."

"How often did they fling?"

"Try not to interrupt me, George: I'll lose my thread. It was an on-off thing. I think he found her relaxing company. She's one of those women who're easy to get on with … you can imagine her … you know, in bed. They'd have the odd drink together, regularly meet one night a week and occasionally a weekend away. He even managed to take her across to France …"

"Cannes?"

"No – Paris. Diana liked Raimond. Said he was a nice sort: very attentive, very charming. The charm us Anglo-Saxons lack, George!"

Bingham had known Brockie for a long time, knew he'd never been unfaithful to his wife and had an almost pathological hatred of criminals: and yet, here he was talking with some admiration of Raimond Chaput, who, if not a criminal, was certainly an adulterer.

Brockie had not had an easy ride with Aileen. She was one of those women who imposed her objections and needs on her husband: he couldn't smoke in the house, was expected to be 'on call' twenty-four hours a day, she didn't like being kept waiting and obliged him to curtail his evenings out to be home by ten o'clock. Yet, he'd stuck with her: shoulder to the wheel, nose to the grindstone. 'You get married and you get on with it,' he'd once said to Bingham.

"What did she have to say about Amanda Chaput?"

"Cold sort – career type. Diana never met her, but didn't like her, anyway."

"Did Raimond talk about his wife to this Diana?"

"Never. It was just impressions she picked up."

"And she never wanted more from him than a good night out and so on?"

"I didn't get the idea she was a marriage breaker, George. Nice woman. She'd been married once, but it came to nothing and her husband had cleared off. Don't get the impression she's common, by the way, George, or rough. We may not approve of her, but she's got what the Americans call 'class'. She could talk about anything under the sun – and intelligently. What are you going to do?"

"I don't know, but at the end of the day there's a mother without her child."

"Let the courts deal with it, George. Stay out of trouble."

"Thanks for your help, Brockie. I now have a clearer picture in my mind of the set up over there. Give my regards to Aileen."

Chapter Nine

THE GRANDMOTHER

Time was running out in Cannes for Lina and Bingham: this was their fourth day and the films of Patrizio and his friends had all been seen and lauded, *Puccini: A Lust for Life* several times, although Bingham was yet to find the opportunity. Public viewings on the beach were not favoured by Patrizio but such was the confusion over badges, invitations and access that he might consider *Cinema de la Plage* as a last resort for his friend's husband.

While he talked lengthily about his next project at breakfast that morning, Bingham's mind was, anyway, elsewhere.

"Go and see her this morning, Bing," said Lina, when they were alone, dressing for the day, "You were miles away at breakfast."

"You'll be OK with Patrizio, will you, if he's 'taken with the moment'?"

"I think I can manage."

*

It was another wonderful day in Cannes: the sun smiled down on them from a sky so blue it was almost mocking its own beauty, the yachts glistened under the relentless cleaning of the deck hands, whites were brilliant, blues were azure. The mountains that shielded the town bristled with the promise of summer and the fruits of autumn: rolling vineyards, olive groves, orange trees, fields of lavender beckoned.

Bingham wandered along the Rue Meynadier and felt at home. He looked up at the little, wrought-iron balconies and the French doors that opened onto them, the windows with their green shutters, the whitewashed walls, the red tiles of the roofs.

He wandered on, almost instinctively, until a winding of narrow streets and passageways led him, again, into the heart of the old town and the address given to him by Raimond Chaput.

"Do come in. I knew you would be early."

The old woman who he now knew was Mathieu's grandmother was standing in her doorway, one leg on the worn step that led up to it and the other on the sill. She gripped the frame of the door with her left hand and held her right across the front of an apron, immaculately pressed, which reminded Bingham of his own grandmother; she was of another time as, perhaps, was Jehane Chaput.

"Sit down, Monsieur, my son said you would come."

She was breathless, not with age but anxiety Bingham thought.

"Please. You will have a coffee."

How many times had he heard that phrase spoken in a French accent that was so comfortable, one of the country rather than the town, the tone of the fields and the bye-ways. He answered, modulating his own voice to suit the small room in which he found himself, his own French finding the right note, one that matched hers.

"Thank you."

The room was furnished, some would say cluttered, with ornaments gathered over a lifetime. China ornaments were placed on a dresser and the window ledge, velvet curtains hung at the windows and cut any winter draughts that might come in under the door, the carpet was patterned with flowers and small tables held knick-knacks. Moving between them was an act of skill and grace.

Bingham heard the old lady moving around in the kitchen: the scrape of a poker in the stove, the slide of a pan across its surface. Jehane Chaput brought his coffee in the traditional bowl and placed it before him as one might present a gift to a god.

"This was our first home," she said, "Mathieu brought me here when we married. Raimond would like me to move in with him but I am comfortable here."

"It's very pleasant," answered Bingham, "and welcoming. A house like this is full of memories. You are from the countryside?"

"Tanneron," she replied, "One day, I shall return there … when the time comes."

Bingham had never heard of the village but saw it in his mind's eye: a quiet place, dusty streets, a bar, a bus once a week to the local market, a church and a graveyard for its people.

"Thank you for seeing me," he said.

Jehane had collapsed into what must have been her usual chair on the other side of the table that bore a heavy velvet cloth topped with an everyday cotton one. He remembered his impression of her that first morning:

the word 'dumped' had come to mind, to describe the way she sat on the bench on the grassy patch outside the Café Potiniere. She was like that now, but her speech wasn't: her speech was that of a woman in quiet control of herself.

"My son fears you will take little Mathieu from us."

"I have no authority to do anything of the kind, Madame Chaput. I was concerned for the boy. That is all. He seemed lost that first morning. He seemed unwilling to talk."

"He has spent most of his time in England."

"It is difficult?"

"Unlike my son, I do not speak your tongue. He is my grandson and we are worlds apart."

"How much have you seen of him?"

"But little ..."

The old lady looked at Bingham, almost begging him to ask another question, but he lifted the bowl of coffee to his lips and waited.

"She should never have discarded my son. He is not a bad man."

It was an odd phrase to choose, *mis au rebut,* to describe Amanda Chaput nee Eaves throwing her husband out.

"They were not together long?" asked Bingham.

"Little Mathieu was barely more than two years old. I had seen my grandson but twice in all that time."

"Had you visited him in his English home?"

"I was not welcome. I sensed I was not welcome."

"It must have been difficult for your son."

"He is not one to cause strife."

"Did little Mathieu visit you here in Cannes?"

"Never. She had no desire to come after the marriage was complete."

"Your son went back and forth to England?"

"There is a small airfield near their home there. Raimond has a light plane. It was not difficult."

"I thought your son brought little Mathieu across on the ferry."

"He thought the airfield would attract too much local attention."

Bingham took another sip from his bowl of coffee.

"She was a woman who wanted things her own way. She could have come to Cannes. Raimond would have provided her with a good life here."

Bingham didn't like to raise the issue of Diana. It seemed to him that Amanda might have been considered as having good reason for 'discarding' this woman's son, at least in Britain.

He began to feel really comfortable in the little sitting room and looked around him. He wondered where little Mathieu would play when he was here. He thought back to a similar sitting room: that of his mother's parents. He remembered sitting in their back parlour on the carpet at his grandad's feet, waiting for the old man to read to him or get out the Ludo board.

"How often does your grandson stay with you?"

"Quite often, at the moment. It will be better when Raimond is settled, and his son is taken into school."

Bingham knew that in France children were gathered into the school system at a very early age, some as early as two years old. He wasn't sure he'd have liked that for his own children: somehow, roaming free under Lina's eye had seemed a better way. At the same time, for working mothers it was a blessing, and Bingham knew that it was a sure way for little Mathieu to learn the language of his father's homeland. He'd seen children who spoke not a word of English become fluent quickly in the embrace of the playground.

"Raimond – your son – is settling down?"

"He has a friend. They have known each other for a long time. You should meet Nicole. She is a good person."

Bingham felt unable to say that he had already met the lady in question and found her cold, at least towards little Mathieu. Her concern had centred on the father. He wondered who would receive the first lick of the ice-cream: her own daughter or the little, English boy.

He felt that Mathieu's well-being would rest very much in the hands of his father who Bingham had liked while, at the same time, considering him an arrogant man. 'I may have been … imprudent' seemed rather an understatement when excusing adultery, and 'the truth is relative. You English think too much of it' verged too near the contemptuous for Bingham's taste.

The room had gone quiet. Why was he here? What was he doing? A mild-mannered man even at the worst of times, Bingham posed a threat to these people; he knew it and hated the fact. That was why he was here: they wanted him persuaded. They wanted him immersed in a warm bath of French culture, soothed and made sodden with another view of the world. But in the Lake District, a mother was pining for her lost child.

"Do you not think," he said, "that your son has brought much of this trouble upon himself?"

"You mean the Englishwoman – the one he sought solace with in your country?"

"Yes – Diana."

"I will make us another coffee, Monsieur Bingham, and perhaps you would like a croissant?"

"Thank you."

No mother would turn her back on her son. Bingham sometimes wondered whether Lina would shelter theirs if either one of them committed a murder: the very moral Lina who never indulged in even the smallest of fibs.

Bingham heard the scrape of the poker and the slide of the pan again and waited. This time, the sounds were accompanied by the opening of a wooden bin and a cupboard door, sounds that even Bingham heard in the quiet of Jehane Chaput's marital home.

The croissant, a plain one, was sliced and buttered and Jehane had placed a pot of jam and a small knife on the wooden tray, a tray marked with the use of decades. She placed a fresh bowl of coffee before Bingham and sagged, once again, onto her chair.

"Monsieur Bingham, you may believe it or not, as you wish, but I was once a very handsome woman, the pick not only of Tanneron but of Cannes itself."

"I have no doubt, Madame. You are a beautiful woman to this day – the eyes, the cheekbones – these are attributes that are never lost."

The old woman smiled, pleased at the compliment. She looked at Bingham, as once she might have looked at a lover, and judged him to be speaking the truth as he saw it.

"My husband, the first Mathieu, was a handsome man, beloved of the ladies, but I won him from them all – the girl from Tanneron. And could I dance! I danced him off his feet. I danced him away from the fine ladies of Cannes and into my arms.

"He was a good man, Mathieu. He worked hard for his family and he kept us in the best circles by his endeavours. He built for us a fine home – for me, for Raimond and for his brother and sisters. We wanted for nothing: the finest clothes he could afford, the best food money could buy.

"And I was a good wife to him. I looked after his home and his children. I reared them to be good people. My daughters made good marriages and live, now, in Paris and Rouen. Raimond's brother, Baptiste, is an architect in Bordeaux. We live far apart but we are still a close family.

"There came a time when I could no longer satisfy Mathieu, when I no longer wanted to satisfy Mathieu, and he was still working so hard for his family. He needed release, and he found it elsewhere. For some women this moment comes late in their marriage, for some early, for others not at all. But Mathieu was a man, a fine man, and I understood."

Bingham couldn't help himself. He'd never heard a woman talk in this way, never imagined he ever would: he had to ask the question.

"Your husband's behaviour must have caused you pain?"

Jehane Chaput must have been near Bingham in age, but she smiled down on him as though he were a small child about to learn an early lesson in life.

"He never humiliated me. He was always discreet. He obeyed the rules."

"Rules?"

"None of the women met our children. They did not touch the family. His liaisons were a thing apart. Only once did he fail me in this way. One of the women took lunch with my grandchildren. My husband had taken her on a business trip to Bordeaux. Baptiste spoke with him, and it did not happen again."

"You never considered divorcing your husband?"

"It is the wife's role to keep the family together. I promised to do that when I married Mathieu and I have kept my promise. Besides, in our family we do not do divorce."

Bingham remembered his feelings when he found out, at the time of the great man's funeral, that the French president, Francois Mitterand, had not only enjoyed a mistress for thirty years but had also fathered what at the time was called a 'lovechild'. Mitterrand's wife and mistress had both attended the funeral. Bingham remembered feeling sorry for the wife and angry at the term 'lovechild'. Surely, he'd thought, the president's other children had also been conceived in love – hadn't they?

Watching Jehane's face and listening to her speak, he now understood at first hand the thoughts that would have been passing through Danielle Mitterand's mind when she stood with her husband's mistress at his funeral.

Bingham didn't agree with any of this licentiousness. How could he, brought up as he had been in the English tradition that sexual love is sublimated in marriage or not at all? But he could see it now from the point of view of these women – the Jehane Chaput's and the Danielle Mitterand's of this world – and he couldn't but admire them.

He ate his croissant and enjoyed his second coffee in silence. They never spoke again until he excused himself to leave.

"I'll see what can be done, Madame Chaput, but you must remember that somewhere in Britain a mother yearns for her child."

"Yes, Monsieur Bingham, I understand."

Chapter Ten

THE MOTHER

The house could only be reached along a winding lane with hedges on either side, and Bingham wondered how Amanda Chaput, nee Eaves, got to work in a hard winter when snow would surely block her way. He wondered, too, how Raimond accustomed himself to living in a spot so isolated and so different to the seaside town he'd lived in since he was a boy.

Bingham wasn't eager to meet little Mathieu's mother. He knew why: he'd come under false pretences. Playing the part didn't trouble him but duplicating the dishonesty already inherent in this relationship did.

He'd talked long and hard with Lina the previous night, the night they'd arrived home from Cannes, and he knew what she thought and what she thought he should do, but Bingham wasn't sure.

Watching *Puccini: A Lust for Life* on their last evening with Patrizio at the *Cinema de la Plage* had not eased Bingham's mind. The composer's own life had been bedevilled with deception, his many affairs leading to the suicide of the young servant girl Puccini's wife had accused, falsely, of having an affair with her husband. 'Oh, what a tangled web we weave, when first we practice to deceive' was one of those warnings issued to Bingham by his mother. He'd never forgotten it; it was like that for boys of his generation.

He left the hire car in the gateway of a field some distance from the house, preferring to walk the final few yards. The gate in question rested heavily in the ground and was well-tangled with grass, and Bingham decided it hadn't been used for years.

He waited awhile, unsure why, and watched the house. It was early morning, the only time Amanda Chaput could offer him, so busy was her day. He had phoned the previous evening from the hotel in Keswick and, standing looking at her house, realized why he was hesitating now that he was here: it had been the tone of her voice.

The house was extensive, sprawled across a garden that lacked a gardener, and surrounded by blackthorn hedges. At one end of the property, overshadowing the gate, was a copse of silver birches.

It was a nice setting, overlooking as it did the fells of the English Lakes, hillsides that sloped away into the morning sun and down to the valley of the River Greta. He'd walked this way once, when younger, and could remember – although he could not now hear – the ripple of water in the becks of the hills.

Bingham paused at the gate but only momentarily. Somehow, the memory of another time had firmed his resolve, reminding him of who he was and what he must do if he was to be honest with himself. He rapped at the door, using the iron knocker that must have been there when the house was built.

The woman who opened the door surprised him: she didn't look Chaput's type at all. He'd imagined an English version of Nicole but this woman wasn't immaculate or what Chaput would have considered feminine. What struck him at once was a ferocity of purpose; that was the phrase that came to his mind. There was no smile on the face, no sign of a welcome. The tight lips were pinched, the eyes almost blank. What she did have in the way of immediate attraction was a mass of wavy, golden-red hair, quite genuine in colour; Bingham couldn't imagine the word 'dye' entering this woman's mind.

"Are you Marlowe?" she asked.

He'd chosen the name out of a sense of devilment because he wanted to keep his own identity out of any further legal action that might be taken, if any was taken at all.

"Yes, and you are Amanda Champoux?"

"Eaves, Amanda Eaves. You've got fifteen minutes, Mr Marlowe, and no more, and it wouldn't be as well that you were wasting my time."

She didn't invite Bingham into her house and so he stepped over the threshold and edged by her in what amounted to a narrow lobby. By a bookcase beyond this a rough-coated dog of the old English sheepdog type lay in the angle between the books and the wall.

"She won't hurt you," said Amanda, "Anyway, she'll be out in the garden very soon. I don't have her in the house when I'm at work, and that's all day."

Bingham knelt and rubbed the dog's chest: they always liked being stroked on the sternum. The dog responded by nuzzling his hand and looked up at him with eyes that he felt were sheepish, almost as though she shouldn't be enjoying herself.

"Well?"

The question was blunt enough. Although he'd have liked a coffee, Bingham didn't expected to be offered one and he wasn't disappointed.

"May I sit down?"

"If you must."

He sat on a hard chair at the kitchen table for the hallway that led off from the narrow lobby drew him directly into the kitchen. Bingham felt in the inside pocket of his jacket for the newspaper clipping that was, he hoped, to establish his credibility.

Amanda glanced at it briefly and tossed it onto the table. She was still standing looking down on him, her back to a pair of French doors that led into the garden.

"Trust an English journalist to get the spelling wrong. It's Chaput, not Champoux. He should have checked. I don't suppose he could be bothered. I reported him to the proprietor. He got a well-deserved ticking off. That brought him down a peg or two.

"Mind you, I'm pleased that mum got my ex with the eggs. It's a pity she felt obliged to admit she shouldn't have done it. It's also a pity he didn't get run over when he darted off across the road. Is this what made you phone me?"

"Yes."

"You want to be paid to find my son?"

"I know France. I thought …"

"My secretary made a few enquiries about you. There's no detective agency in this country under that name or one with a Marlowe attached to it."

"I don't run an agency, but I've had some luck in the past finding missing people."

"What makes you think you can find my son any more successfully than our inefficient police officers?"

"I don't operate under the same restrictions."

Bingham's stance had attracted her attention and he waited for a response. He no longer felt under the pressure of having to complete his business in fifteen minutes or threatened by wasting her time.

He'd met her sort many times: parents who charged into school bristling with indignation, only to leave pacified once they thought they'd got their way. He wondered what she was like to work with, how colleagues responded to what appeared to be her natural hostility rather than an assumed strategy to deal with a stranger.

He hadn't expected to be invited but would have come anyway: a little boy's future was at stake, and Bingham had taken a liking to the child, a liking that was instinctive, the instinct to protect being strong in a normal person.

He tried to picture this woman with Chaput. He tried to imagine them strolling arm in arm along La Croisette. What did they talk about, what did they have in common: Chaput with his easy manner, his wife with her intensity? Bingham was quite prepared to accept that opposites attract but wasn't so sure they'd stick together. Chaput strolled, she bristled: nothing but an edgy walk seemed likely. Did they look at the boats, did they discuss the town?

"How well do you know France?"

Was she hooked? Bingham didn't think so: a naturally suspicious woman would not be drawn in so easily. She was testing him.

"I understand from the court proceedings that your husband came from Cannes. I know the town well. I was there only two years ago at the film festival and stayed on for an extended holiday."

"Oh, you mean the annual jamboree of the idle and the workshy. It must sicken the local people to have their town swarming with the noisy, the unkempt and the disreputable for two weeks every year. I wonder they don't complain."

"They're French," replied Bingham, choosing his words deliberately, "and they see things differently to us."

"You can say that again!"

"You must have spent some time in Cannes yourself."

"Obviously, since I married a Frenchman."

"Yes, of course. It was a country that was attractive to you at one time."

He left his last sentence hanging in the air: it might have been a comment or a question, relying on his tone of voice, and he wanted Amanda Chaput to decide for herself, wanted to provoke her without appearing inquisitive.

"It's a painful memory, one I'd rather not dwell on. Chaput was a man of importance in the town when we met. Little did I know how things might turn out."

"You were not familiar with the French and their ways."

"Do you like the French?"

"I can take them or leave them," replied Bingham, considering his comment less a lie than merely part of a necessary subterfuge, "You had a house there?"

"Chaput may not know it, but I still have a house there – his house! I'm having my share of that – don't doubt it!"

Bingham didn't.

"Chaput seemed suitable. He earned a very good living and said he could make a woman happy."

She looked menacingly at Bingham, daring him to defy or mock her.

"You kept your own, thriving business going here in Keswick?"

"I had no intention of ever being dependent on a man. I've seen too much of them. What makes you think my son is in France?"

Bingham had been waiting for the question. A woman as sharp as Amanda Chaput must have detected this weakness in his persona almost as soon as he offered his services, and she'd waited her moment to ask, waited to catch him off-guard.

"It was mentioned in the newspaper clipping and my colleague made enquiries."

"Colleague? There's more than one of you?"

"There has to be for the kind of work we do."

"Where did you make your *enquiries*?"

She stressed the word, imbuing it with a distaste that suggested such activity might almost verge on the pornographic.

"Here," replied Bingham, "in Keswick."

"You had no right ..."

"We were sent the clipping by 'a concerned individual' – that's the phrase often used by people who want to help but don't want to be involved – and she felt the little boy might be distressed."

"She?"

"The tone of the note attached to the clipping suggested a woman. I might be wrong."

"But you don't know who she is?"

"No," replied Bingham, thinking that since she didn't exist this was not surprising.

Amanda Chaput sat down on the opposite side of the table, a move Bingham had wanted and expected. For the first time since he'd arrived, he felt sorry for the woman.

"I don't approve of people prying into my business."

"In a small town like Keswick, I'm afraid you have to expect it."

"Who *helped* you with your *enquiries*?"

Again, the emphasis suggesting another, dirtier world than the one Amanda Chaput inhabited.

"I'd rather not say, Mrs Chaput …"

"Eaves – I've gone back to my maiden name, understandably considering the circumstances. I want to know who these people are."

"It's confidential, as is my conversation with you. Someone who has a junior reporter disciplined for misspelling a name is, I think, likely to take reprisals against anyone helping us with our enquiries."

"Enquiries you had no business to make."

"That's true, but we wanted to be as well-informed as possible should you choose to let us help you find your son."

"And if I don't choose?"

"Everything is shredded."

"I may choose to shred you, Mr Marlowe."

"We've broken no law. We're merely offering to help."

Amanda Eaves sat quietly for a while and, watching her, Bingham felt another surge of pity. Despite her hostility, she was a woman whose only child had been taken from her and who knew the French authorities would be dragging their feet on the matter. Eventually, she spoke, the words drawn from her unwillingly.

"I suppose your *colleague* met *her*?"

"Yes, we met Diana Hart."

"Hmm! Hartless would be more suitable. I'd rather not say how much suffering she caused me. I've never met her – I don't want to – but I saw her once. You know the sort. Tart from the feet up. Chaput had no business getting married if he preferred that sort of woman. They're easy enough to find anywhere, any street corner, any pub or club, even in the workplace nowadays.

"When a man isn't capable of being faithful, he should stick with the whores of this world. A man like that has no pride and he takes away what a woman once had. I was respected in this town. I'd built up an estate agency that was a household name for its efficiency and fairness. As you may know, estate agents aren't generally admired in this world. We're looked upon as a necessary, money-grabbing evil but Eaves Estate Agents were esteemed throughout the Lakes."

"I'm sure they still are. Were you the one who asked for the divorce?"

"What do you think!"

"I have to ask, if we're to help find your son."

"Don't be too quick to stroke your wallet, Mr Marlowe. I haven't said I want your help."

"True. I was trying to build up a picture of your husband."

"*Ex*-husband. Chaput kidnapped our son from the nursery with the help of his tart. They're being sued for every penny they have now. I'm going to close them down if it's the last thing I do."

"Was it a good nursery?" asked Bingham, unable to help himself.

"What's that got to do with it?"

"If it's closed, the children who've been going there will suffer."

Amanda Eaves looked at Bingham as though he'd just dropped in from a parallel universe. He saw in her eyes that she understood exactly what he meant. In the same instant, the expression changed: the nursery had betrayed her and that was enough to justify her intention.

"I once closed an Indian restaurant, Mr Marlowe."

"I'm sorry?"

"They served me a curry I considered to be badly prepared. The manager disagreed and had the temerity to suggest he might know more about curries than I did. When I got home I sent a text to everyone I know, and that's a lot of people in a small town. Word spread, and he was out of business within months."

This isn't a woman you'd want to cross, thought Bingham, and wondered why she'd not bypassed the official channels already. She must know her son was most likely to be in Cannes somewhere. He was relieved he'd left the hire car, booked in his own name, at the bottom of the lane, hopefully hidden from view by the blackthorn hedges.

"No one knows what I've suffered at Chaput's hands, and I'll take him for every penny he owns but I don't want any maintenance payments from him. The monthly bank transfer would make me vomit.

"I'll put my son through school. I'll see he has a decent English education. There are plenty of good boarding schools around, and it will easier for me if he's looked after during the week. I work long hours, often at odd times."

Bingham could appreciate that boarding school would best suit Amanda Eaves, but would it best suit her son? He thought of the little boy playing with his car on the patch of grass outside the Café Potiniere. He was one of those children often described as 'sensitive': not that the term didn't apply to all children, but it had a special meaning for some.

"France will corrupt him as it corrupted his father," continued Amanda, as though reading Bingham's thoughts, and then added, "I won't let Chaput take him away from me. Chaput! Hmm! It would surprise me if he hadn't picked a French tart already … However did I become involved with a man like him – let alone allow him to marry me!"

If there was such a thing as quiet hysteria, Amanda Eaves was its most accomplished exponent. Bingham didn't believe she could be in any state other than one of torment; he'd expected to see that tight lower lip tremble, at least, and wouldn't have been surprised at the occasional sob, but nothing came from her other than the abuse of all and sundry.

"You've made no attempt as yet to retrieve your son, other than through the proper channels?"

"What do you mean?

Even the simplest question aroused suspicions; here was a woman who trusted no one.

"You're clearly a determined woman, Mrs Eaves, and I am a little surprised that you've not employed someone like me earlier to look into this abduction for you."

"I have no more faith in people like you, Mr What-ever-your-name-is, than in the forces that call themselves Law and Order."

"It may take years to resolve this through the courts."

"It *will* take years …"

"How did you find your ex-husband's family?"

"What has that got to do with anything?"

"It might help to know should you wish us to take on the case."

"The father's dead and the mother, by the look of her, should be. A great lump of French fat, irretrievably Catholic."

"You were married in France?"

"They gave me no choice. It was a mistake, but I was ..."

She almost blushed. Bingham could have finished the sentence for her: the word 'besotted' came to mind.

"Her conscience cannot be clear."

"In what way?"

"They're big family people aren't they – or supposed to be – the French. I wonder how she sleeps at night knowing a mother is without her child."

Not easily, thought Bingham.

"If you don't mind my saying so, Mrs Eaves, your bitterness will wear you down ..."

"I do mind you saying so. It remains none of your business. I haven't had a day off work since I bought the agency from the wet-nosed, previous owner – my employer, for my sins. One of those men who sit there expecting the cherries to fall into their lap without shaking the tree. He was running the agency into the ground through sheer idleness. He passes by, occasionally, and cannot believe what he's seeing. Ever seen envy in a man's eyes? You'll see it in his."

Listening to her, Bingham wondered whether she and Chaput ever argued. He couldn't believe otherwise and thought the rows must have been virulent. It was impossible to have a reasonable disagreement with someone who was always right, and he didn't doubt that Amanda Chaput, now Eaves, was always right.

What would the rows have been about? Visits to his family? Where might they set up a permanent home for little Mathieu? Chaput's mother? Chaput's father – had Amanda found out about him? Who paid what bills for where? The list was endless; if a couple wanted to disagree, finding a subject was never a problem.

He wondered about Amanda's background. What had her home life been like? It isn't everyone's mother who will wait patiently outside a courtroom to throw eggs at an ex-husband. Like mother, like daughter?

Bingham didn't know, but he'd heard enough. Some years before, a friend of his who, following a divorce, had been separated from his only daughter for several years had, eventually, been reunited with his child. At a High Court hearing, the judge ruled that the child had been manipulated by the mother into believing her father did not want her. The girl would "rant" about her father, and the judge decided she should be removed from the mother's care. The local county council took responsibility for the child and it was their duty to provide social workers who would "facilitate" the girl's return to her father. In the end, this was successful; but Bingham was left wondering what underlying harm had been done in the meantime.

"I shall be going, now, Mrs Eaves," he said.

"I haven't told you whether or not I require your services yet, Mr Marlowe."

"I didn't come to find that out," he replied, "I came to decide whether or not I wanted the case."

He didn't wait for her retort but got up from the table and made his way through the hall. Bingham looked down at the dog, as he passed.

"She looks sad," he said.

"Hmm! She was Chaput's idea when he was going through his 'I-love-everything-English' phase. She's a mongrel, of course, like him, but there's a sheepdog in her somewhere."

Bingham knelt and stroked the dog gently on her breast, thinking to himself that she deserved a better home than the one shared with Amanda Eaves.

Chapter Eleven
THE WIFE

"We've a new family member," said Bingham, pushing open the bottom half of the stable door that led into their kitchen.

Lina looked up from the bowl where she was kneading dough, her hands covered in flour and watched as her three other dogs made their various moves to greet the stranger: Pippa the Labrador with a lick, George the West Highland White with a wander round and Ben the Cairn with a slight, warning growl. The Old English mongrel stood quietly accepting the inspection, her eyes on Bingham.

"Meet Mollie," he said, quietly to the other dogs, "She's here to stay."

His tone was everything as far as the dogs were concerned: a low, crooning sound of warning and welcome.

Over a cup of tea, he related his meeting with Amanda Eaves.

"She simply drove off," he said, as he came to the end of his story, "leaving me and Mollie in the road outside her house. She said I'd held her up enough already and that we'd better call a taxi, if we could find a taxi that would take a dog."

"What a horrible woman. It was lucky you had your hire car down the lane. How much did you give her for Mollie?"

"A hundred pounds. She said she'd made a profit on the deal."

Lina looked at her husband but said nothing else, although Bingham knew she'd feel obliged to do so later, in the quiet of the evening after they'd walked the dogs and settled Mollie onto her new bed in Bingham's study, where he planned to spend this first night with her.

It was a warm spring, hoping for a warm summer. The barley was already ripening in the fields as they strolled hand in hand, while the terriers ran wild, sniffing for rabbits in the hedgerows and the Labrador went back and forth, rounding them up, always returning to Bingham and Lina, fulfilling her role as the enforcer, the one who kept the pack together. Already, she and Mollie were nuzzling each other and rubbing noses.

Bingham and Lina were sitting at a small dining table on the Italianate terrace, created by her mother so many years before and now tended lovingly by Lina, each enjoying a glass of cold Orvieto, before Lina spoke.

"I know what you're thinking, Bing – the boy will be better off with an adulterous father and his strange milieu than with an angry mother – but I think you may be wrong."

"She was angry at everything and everybody."

"But she is the boy's mother."

"The biological right."

"Yes. You cannot get away from the fact that she carried the child within her for nine months, gave birth to him and suckled him when he was a baby. A child is always drawn back to that time in their lives, a time forgotten that is always remembered, however instinctively. If our children had ever had to choose between you and me, what would have been their choice?"

"You, and I'm happy it should be so; but I'm not happy with the idea of telling Amanda Eaves what I know, not happy with providing her with ammunition for the custody battle."

"You think the father has a chance of keeping his son because by the time the courts get around to deciding the matter, little Mathieu will already have settled into his new life."

"Yes."

"He will seek out his mother one day. There is always that pull of nature."

"Hopefully when her animosity can no longer do him any harm."

"The rights of the child always come first," said Lina.

"Yes. I thought you really agreed with me."

"I didn't say so, Bing, and you know it."

The darkness had closed in before they decided to call it a day, and a barn owl flew across from the old farm buildings by the pond. Bingham looked at Lina, although he couldn't see her, and thanked the stars, not for the first or even the hundredth time, for the luck they'd brought him.

Spring 2019

www.ingramcontent.com/pod-product-compliance
Lightning Source LLC
Chambersburg PA
CBHW022032170626
46808CB00003B/1160